A Thug Saved My Heart 4

D1568457

By: S.Yvonne

Please feel free to stay connected with me:

Facebook Personal Page:
https://www.facebook.com/shalaine.powell

Facebook Author Page:
https://www.facebook.com/author.syvonne/

Facebook Reading Group:
https://www.facebook.com/groups/506882726157516/?ref=share

Instagram Author Page:
https://instagram.com/authoress_s.yvonne?igshid=191pn9mnx922b

Recap

Kimberly 'Kim' Laws

I could tell from the moment I got on the phone with LeLe just how serious this was. I knew this was coming one day but I wasn't prepared. I was finally feeling at peace and enjoying my baby. I named him Majestic after his dad but gave him my last name. Majestic Jr. was the spitting image of his dad. Hell, we didn't even need a DNA to prove that. The tears rolled down my eyes as I hurried to put me and the baby a bag together. It had been seven weeks since I delivered and my baby only had to stay in the hospital two of those weeks. He was so strong and had been such a fighter. I couldn't leave him behind cause I didn't trust anyone to keep him and at the same time; this was the time for Majestic to know he had a son.

I couldn't live with him even killing off Trell cause he didn't deserve that. Nobody deserved that cause this was all on me. When I packed the bags and knew that I had Enfamil and everything for the baby, I packed up the car and then ran back inside for a few more things before locking up. I looked slightly different than the last time they'd seen me. I no longer had the fit body. Instead, I had the 'mommy' body and had gotten thick in all the right places. I chopped all of my long hair off as well and was wearing a short cut now. I just felt like it was appropriate since I was trying to turn over a new leaf but just like the devil and just like Karma, they always showed up and when we least expected it.

I had to make sure my baby was fed and feeling good and comfortable before I hit the road. Me on the other hand I couldn't even eat at all. My stomach was in knots, and fresh tears blurred my vision. I wasn't the same person they knew before I left Miami. I had learned so much about myself and come to certain terms with a lot of things about my life. I took my baby with me to church every Sunday and took an hour out of my day to read the bible every Wednesday night. If I had to leave this world I didn't wanna leave with all these demons.

I looked back at my sleeping baby. He'd brought so much joy to my life in such a little period of time. I didn't think it was possible to love somebody this much but here I was doing it and doing all by myself too. Emily and Karter helped out from time-to-time but for the most part they gave me my space so I could figure this mommy thing out my own way. Karter had told me that our mama called her asking about my son but I told her she better not tell that bitch nothing else about me, shit, tell her I disappeared. I didn't care what she told her to be honest. I just wanted her to stay far away from me.

I was making sure I went speed limit while driving cause I never wanted to drive to fast with the baby in the car and I needed some time to just think. I thought about everything I could possibly do. Emily called me multiple times and I didn't answer until I was halfway to Miami. I ignored her mostly because I knew she would try to talk me out of going or she would've at least tried to make me leave my baby with Karter and her nanny and I wasn't doing that. I needed Majestic to look in this child's eyes.

"Hello?" I finally answered with my voice cracking.

"Hey, I'm here at your apartment to drop some things off for the baby. Where are you guys?" She asked. "Are you crying?"

Silence.

"Kim, where are you?" She asked again.

I took a deep breath and told her the truth. "I'm headed home... back to Miami."

"Wait!" She yelled. "Kim..."

I cut her off and hung up powering my phone off. My mind couldn't be changed. This is what I had to do and if I had to die in the process then so be it. Sometimes this is just how the tables turned. Fuck it. "See you soon Miami." I whispered to myself. See you real soon.

Chapter 1

Kimberly 'Kim' Laws

The closer I got to Miami, the more a sense of calmness overcame me. As soon as I got off the turnpike on my exit, I pulled over and called LeLe. "I'm here." I told her. Where can we meet?"

"I think I know where he is. It's an Industrial area on 71st by the warehouses. Meet me there in fifteen minutes. If he does anything to my brother, I'mma kill you Kim and that's a promise." She said coldly hanging up in my face. I couldn't even blame her for being mad with me or feeling the way that she felt cause Lord knows I'd feel the same exact way if the shoe were on the other foot. I looked back at the rear facing car seat and then got out to grab my baby. My heart fluttered watching him squirm in his sleep so I could change his diaper and feed him before he started cutting up.

As unruly as I was, I was surprised that he was such a good baby. He hardly gave me any problems at all and that's how I liked it. He was such a sweet little bundle of joy. When I was finished, I put him back and then I just sat and thought for a minute. I needed to call Majestic myself. It took everything in me to build up the balls to do it, but before I just showed up, I needed to do this. I took a deep breath and dialed his number. "Who the fuck is this?" His deep voice growled into the phone.

My heart started beating fast as hell. "Majestic." His name rolled off of my tongue like a snake spitting venom. I didn't want him to do anything crazy to nobody because of my fucked up ways. I had damaged him in the worst way but I knew somewhere in there he still had a good heart. Just like me, Majestic didn't react well to hurt. Just like me, he did dumb ass shit too. "It's me, it's Kim. Listen to me, please…"

He cut me off. "Is it true?" He asked. "That's all I wanna know. Is it true?"

"I… um… I know where you are. I'm coming to see you. Please don't do anything crazy." I was damn near begging by now. "Just let me explain."

"You got ten minutes to get here." He hung up in my face.

I didn't even want LeLe to get involved in this mess, but I knew that she would still come even if I told her not to cause Trell was involved.

In exactly ten minutes, I was pulling up to the warehouse that LeLe wanted me to meet her at. I saw her Nissan backed in on the side of the building. As soon as she saw me, she hopped out of the car wearing some long, black spandex, a black hoodie, and some rider boots. Her hair was pulled up in a sloppy bun and she looked as if she was ready for war. Her eyes were focused on me the entire time she made her way to my car.

"Hurry the fuck up Kim." She growled as I rushed to the back of my car opening the door.

"I'm coming." I told her. I hurriedly tried to grab my baby. I could hear the gravel and rocks' crunching underneath her boots, and the closer she got it was giving me anxiety. Junior started whining when I took him out of the car throwing a blanket over him making sure he was comfortable and all covered up. Even in this moment and the extent of the situation, I only wanted to make sure that he was okay. "Shhh, mommy got you." I rocked him before closing the door and hitting the lock button. "I'm ready." I told LeLe.

She tilted her head sideways and snarled. "Mommy?" She asked.

I nodded my head.

She chuckled and let out a deep evil laugh. "I loss my baby because of your evil ass and you done ran off to have a baby Kim? So who is this child's daddy?" She asked with a raised eyebrow.

I felt like shit. I wanted to vomit. I still couldn't believe I had done all of that shit. I didn't expect her to feel any sympathy at all for me because I had a child of my own. Because of me, she missed out on being a mommy with the man who she loved the most. "LeLe, I wish I could apologize a million and one times. I would give anything to take everything back, even if I have to lose my life in the process. I swear to God." I felt the tears in my eyes but I didn't allow them to fall cause I knew that wasn't gonna change shit at all.

"It's way too late for apologies." She had the same blank stare on her face and pointed to my baby again. "Who is the daddy."

"Majestic." I told her.

She sucked her teeth. "You's just one low down dirty ass bitch Kim." She shook her head. "Couldn't have one brother so you bore the child of the next."

"It wasn't supposed to happen this way LeLe." I said in my defense although I really didn't have one. I looked at the warehouse. "Let's go and get Trell."

She turned around and led the way as I followed closely behind. I kept imagining the different ways I'd die. Like was this a set up? Would Majestic kill me? Would LeLe do it? Is Trell even okay? These were all the thoughts going through my head all at one. LeLe had to knock twice. When the door did open, it seemed more like a switch controlled it or button opposed to someone letting us in cause we were greeted with nobody at all. "Hellooooo!" LeLe rushed in. "Trell!" She stood in the middle of the warehouse yelling. "Majestic! I've got your bitch out here! Now where the fuck is my brother!" She yelled.

Majestic slowly walked from the back of the warehouse as the light shined down on his beautiful face causing my heart to drop since I saw so much of Junior in him. I swallowed and took a deep breath while squeezing my baby tight; not enough to hurt him though. I just wanted him to feel his mama's love just in case he was never able to feel it again. I remained strong though. I wasn't going to beg. I came here to handle my business. My eyes reverted from his face down to his hands, they were empty but I knew better. I knew he was carrying.

LeLe slowly looked at me. "Tell him Kim! Tell him everything." She demanded looking like a deranged woman. Not the sweet girl that I knew.

"You ran away and had a fucking baby? I know God aint bless yo crazy ass with no baby Kim. Why the fuck you come here with a baby? That ain't gone save you." He growled but I could see the hurt in his eyes.

"I ran away cause I found out I was pregnant and I wanted to get clean and get my life together Majestic."

Before I could continue he grabbed a handful of my hair causing me to yell out in pain but he wouldn't let go and I refused to drop my baby. With a handful of my little short cut hair in his hands, he brought his lips down to my ear causing an vibration as he spoke. "Don't fuckin' lie to me again Kim. Now what happen?"

It would've been much easier to talk if he wasn't yanking my hair causing my head to be in a very uncomfortable position. "LeLe, I'm begging, please get my son. I don't wanna drop him and I don't want him getting hurt. Please." I cried. That's the only reason I had any tears at this particular moment. There was an awkward silence and I just knew she wasn't going to get him. At the same time, I knew LeLe wasn't a monster either. I felt a sigh of relief when I felt her reach for him.

Majestic slung me to the ground causing me to fall on my bare knees. It hurt so badly that I was almost sure that he broke something or fractured it one. I didn't know where the blood on my leg was coming from but I didn't have time to try to figure it out either. Time was running out. I felt an excruciating pain in my ankle and grabbed it. "Majestic." I heaved in and out fighting through the pain as he hovered over me. I had never been afraid of him up until this point. "I fucked up. You know me, you know my struggle. You know things about me that I hadn't even told my own friends. What I didn't tell you about was me being with Malik before he got with LeLe. It was nothing, we were just fucking but he didn't want me and he made that very clear. When he chose LeLe, I was jealous Majestic. I hated him for that after already being through so much rejection. The night they had the accident it wasn't LeLe's fault, so please stop hating her." I begged with snot now running down my nose. "It was me who spiked the drinks. I didn't wanna kill nobody, I only wanted to hurt them real bad for hurting me!" I blurted it out feeling a weight lift from my chest.

I could sense the hurt bouncing off the walls in this room. Majestic was blankly staring at me. Slowly, he pulled his gun from the small of his waist and cocked it. I knew Majestic cared more for me than what he admitted. I saw the hurt and frustration in his eyes. I squeezed my eyes tight when I felt him put the tip of the gun to the side of my head. "Wait! You gone kill her right here? In front of me?" LeLe asked stopping him.

I had to think and I had to think quick but this was my opportunity to say something. "Wait! Please!" I cried. "My son! He's yours Majestic! I had planned on coming clean to everybody and I found out I was pregnant first. I took the sucker way out and I just ran away. I ran to get clean so I could stop snorting that shit. I ran to give my baby a chance but I always knew I'd have to come back." I cried while still holding my ankle and rocking back and forth. Immediately Junior started crying as if he knew something was wrong with his mama. Or maybe it was my voice. Still on the ground I reached for him while staring LeLe in the eyes. "Please, give him to me. Please." I asked defeated.

She looked from me to the baby and passed me the baby. I grabbed him and rocked him back and forth ignoring my own pain making sure that I didn't try to get up. At this point I wasn't even sure it was possible. I didn't even realize until LeLe gave me the baby that she had tears in her eyes as well. "She told you everything you need to know Majestic! Now where's my brother?" LeLe asked looking him in the face.

"Let me see his face." He ignored LeLe staring down at me. I didn't want to expose my baby to him with that look in his eyes because I didn't know what he had on his mind. "NOW!" His voice echoed through the warehouse causing me to jump and my baby to whine and squirm. Since LeLe hadn't removed his blanket or bothered to really look at him not even she knew what he looked like.

I removed the blanket from his face. "He's yours Majestic, and he's 7 weeks old. I had him early, he was a little premature but he was strong and he made it. He looks exactly like you and your brother." I cried. "Kill me if you want to but please don't kill him. He's innocent."

I heard LeLe gasp lightly as she took a peek and immediately covered her mouth. The tears that poured from her eyes were for her own child that she loss. I could imagine a little baby that looked exactly like this one. She shook her head. "This bitch isn't lying. She's telling the truth."

Majestic hesitated and frowned his face like he was examining him. I could tell by the look in his eyes that he knew I was telling the truth. DNA didn't need to be done to confirm this was his baby. He was staring into tiny little eyes that looked exactly like his. He saw it and I know he did.

Chapter 2

Leandra 'LeLe' Wells

"I can't believe this shit." I wiped the corners of my eyes. With everything in me I hated Kim. At the same time, I felt for this child that she brought into her fucked up life. God couldn't come down on a cloud himself and make me believe that Kim had changed. Maybe she did change, I just couldn't see past that right now. There was no denying that looking into this child's face that he was Majestic's. The baby looked exactly like him and nobody could tell me any different. "It's your baby Majestic." I told him. "Great! Congrats! I don't give a fuck what you do to Kim's ass. Just give me my fucking brother." I demanded. "Trellll!" I called his name out again.

Without looking at me and with his eyes fixated on the baby and Kim, he replied with so much coldness in his voice. "Trell ain't here. I know I'm a fucked up nigga but I ain't that fucked up. Nigga ain't no fuckin' snake and despite how fucked up I felt bout you; I couldn't do my homie like that. Thought about it." He shrugged. "But nah."

I was beyond fucking confused right now and the fact that my phone kept blowing up really baffled me although I knew it was my family calling out of concern. "What?" I frowned. "What the fuck do you mean he isn't here? He is missing! We haven't seen him! You said you had him!"

"I said what I needed to fuckin' get you here. I wanted to kill yo muthafuckin' ass. That ain't got shit to do with Trell them. That nigga went out of town to hit a big ass lick cause he needed the bread and he ain't answering cause he knows somebody was gone try to stop him and he needed to be focused. Take it how you want. That was my opportunity to get yo ass alone. Get a fuckin' apology before puttin' yo ass in the grave right next to Malik."

I couldn't believe this shit. This wasn't what I expected at all. Majestic hated me that much he would do anything just to turn my world upside down. "Nigga! I didn't do it!" I wanted to haul off and slap his ass. "Your baby mama just admitted to that shit! You're a damn lie about Trell!"

He slowly pulled his phone from his pocket and put it on speaker. I couldn't believe that Trell actually picked up. "Assalamualaikum nigga." Majestic said into the phone.

"Mualaikumsalam. I'm headed back now. Fuck wit'chu when I get back." Trell hung up the phone. I couldn't even believe this shit. I couldn't do anything besides shake my muthafuckin' head and I was so glad nobody knew what I was up to even coming here. Me getting anybody else involved would've caused an entire blood bath. Kim still sat on the floor trying to console the baby at this point. She wasn't even shy about popping her breast nipple in his mouth in order to get him to calm down again.

I looked at her with pitty. It made me sick to my stomach watching her with her baby knowing she made me lose mine. Kim didn't even look the same. She looked healthier. She looked nurturing. She looked really good but most of all she looked like… a mother. She ignored her own pain and she even ignored Majestic still hovering over her to make sure her baby was okay. Deep down inside, I wanted to kill her ass.

"What do you wanna do with her?" Majestic asked me snapping out of his own thoughts. "Ion give a fuck if you mad. We all got put in a fucked up position but since she caused both of our hurt, it's yo call. I'll put a bullet in this bitch head right now. I'll raise my son. Fuck her."

I stared at Kim and sighed. "Ion know what I want to do with her." The bigger part of me says let God handle it. The other part of me wanted to bury her ass. I wasn't a killer but Kim had taken so much away from me, including my life. "I'm not sure yet. I'll let you know." I told him leaving him with Kim. I had to get out of this fucking warehouse. It was making me sick. Literally; I felt sick as if I was going to pass the fuck out. The most important thing was getting home to let everyone know that not only was I okay but so was Trell.

Despite the situation, I would never forgive Ms. Jones for the shit she said about my brother cause obviously she wasn't aware that Majestic didn't really have Trell. She was just going along with whatever he had told her, but it was like sugar on her tongue when she thought Majestic was really about to kill Trell. 'A kid for a kid' is what she said and I would never forget that. Fuck her. I never thought I would say something like that about Malik's mama, but I hoped Majestic told her sick ass the truth. She could never even come back to me with any apologies. She meant exactly what she said and that showed me a lot about her character.

I pulled up in the driveway of the house and was greeted with my mama smoking a cigarette when I walked up on the porch. She wore bags under her eyes and I could tell she'd been crying. "Trell is fine mama." I told her.

She took a deep breath and sighed and then pulled on her cigarette again and released a cloud of smoke. "Ya'll fucking kids are gonna drive me to drugs next." She said shaking her head looking up at the sky since the sun was setting.

I didn't have time to argue with her about this. Hell, Trell nearly gave me a heart attack and he needed to explain himself about what happened when he got back. I called Leon when I got to my room because I knew he was on edge and probably waiting to get a call so he can get his hands dirty if need be. When I told him that Trell was okay he had no questions for me, even when I tried to explain. Seemed like that's all he wanted to hear. He didn't even finish talking to me. One minute he was on the phone and the next, Kevin was on the line. "He hasn't drink or eaten shit all day. Thank God Trell is okay." Kevin expressed his gratitude over the phone. "He's pouring a drink right now. He has all kind of guns and shit. I had no idea."

"Yeah well, I'm not surprised." I told him. I was just frustrated at this point. I also had Kim's bitch ass on my mind. Torn in between going back and putting a bullet in her damn head or just letting it go. I knew one thing was for sure, and that is that Majestic was going to give her hell for now.

When I hung up with Kevin, I checked my voicemail and had one from my bitch ass manager at Taco Bell since I didn't show up to work and bailed on my shift. I couldn't believe his stank ass fired me over fucking voicemail. "Fuck!" I flopped down on the damn bed. I couldn't afford to take a fucking pay cut right now. McDonald's just wasn't enough money to make it come out right. I took a deep breath and just exhaled to calm myself down. I just wanted to fucking scream. "FUCK!" I yelled again.

George knocked on my room door before opening it. "Leandra, that's twice now. I ignored the first one." He warned. "Now your mama told me Trell was okay. I don't even want to know what happened or where his ass has been. It's over now calm your young ass nerves child. Your birthday is tomorrow. Get out of that funk." He closed the door leaving me in my thoughts.

I had actually forgotten all about my birthday. I hadn't made any plans either. Birthdays are the worse days for me so I honestly tried not to think about it. In prison, the few chicks I did fuck with would always try to do something to make it special. No matter what we had for dinner they would always make sure I had a cupcake that they made out of our snacks. Still, it wasn't the same even then. I didn't even wanna celebrate in prison either though cause it was like pouring salt on an open wound. A wound that would never completely close as long as I was alive.

I laid back on my bed and almost went the fuck off when my door opened again. Without looking, I assumed it was George again. "I didn't even say shit else George."

"It ain't George bitch." Abbey said standing over me wearing a look of frustration and anger. "You had us all worried just running off like that LeLe. Where the fuck did you go?" She asked. "Any word from Trell?"

"Trell is fine." I mumbled.

I could see she didn't like that. "So he's fine? Ain't shit wrong with him and he couldn't even call nobody? Nahhhh.... This nigga was with a bitch. I told him to clean his shit up not fucking disappear and go fuck on somebody's daughter for the last time."

I shook my damn head. "I don't think he's been with a bitch. When you see him then you let him explain. I told you, ion want no parts in this shit here."

"You right." She nodded her head piercing her lips together trying to refrain from saying shit else about it. Had it been any other nigga outside of Trell, we would've been straight dogging his ass but I wasn't gonna say anything extra. Abbey sat on the foot of the bed. "So where have you been?"

"I went to see Ms. Jones but fuck her. I'm done with that lady. I went to tell her the truth and she showed me her true colors so fuck it and fuck her too. Oh, and Kim is here. I made her tell Majestic the truth."

"Hol' up bitch come again, say what?" She asked with an uncertain frown on her face.

"Yeah, he knows the truth. Would you believe she's clean and she had a baby from Majestic? That's why she ran away."

"A baby from Majestic?! Jesus Christ this shit is a whole fucking circus. So where she at now? Is she alive? He gone let her live? Like what ya'll gone do? When the fuck did she even get pregnant?"

I shrugged. On God I had thought of multiple ways I could kill her ass without feeling bad about it. "I don't give a fuck what he does to her. I hope he tortures her ass until we figure this out. I'm not a fucking snitch and I don't wish jail on nobody but her ass needs to pay."

"You know it's a matter of time before Karter them calls looking for her LeLe."

"I don't care, I hope Majestic figures all of that out."

"And the baby?" She asked with one eyebrow raised.

I sighed. "I feel sorry for that baby because he's innocent." I sighed. "I just don't even know and this is too much to think about right now. On top of that Taco Bell fired my ass for a no call no show. I gotta get me another job."

"No." She shook her head. "Maybe this is the push you need to go ahead and open your restaurant. Fuck Taco Bell."

I thought about what Abbey was saying. I hadn't even gotten the chance to tell her what Trey had done for me. Speaking of Trey. I hadn't even heard from him since I told him I'd call him back and he's only text me once since then to ask if I was okay. I should've already known he was the type of nigga that wasn't gonna blow any bitch up or run any bitch down. Still, I did need to let him know everything was okay. "Trey took me to a place. I'm gonna see about buying it. I guess I'm just afraid of not having any money left once I spend it on everything."

"You have to spend money to make money girl. Don't be afraid to invest in yourself." Abbey suggested. "Just do it."

"I guess you right." I told her taking a long deep breath. I looked down at my flashing phone. It was Karter. I ignored it.

Abbey's phone started to ring next. "Was that Karter?" She asked.

"Yep."

"What should I say?"

"Tell her the truth, you haven't seen Kim. Technically, you haven't."

Abbey stepped out of the room to take the call. I used this time to call Trey back.

"Hey Trey." I said as soon as he picked up.

"Everything aiight with the fam?" He asked in his deep voice.

"Yeah, Trell is okay. Everything is okay." I told him. "I just wanted to call you back and let you know that."

"Good." He told me. "I'mma come check you tonight shorty."

"I'll be here." I told him hanging up with a half smile on my face. I couldn't wait to see his mysterious ass. The less he told me, the more I wanted to know. I was also obsessed with the way he picked my mind. The nigga was very much intriguing. After hanging up with him, I went to find Abbey's ass but I was greeted with Trell walking through the front door instead. This muthafucka had some explaining to do!

Chapter 3

Abbey Daniels

I hated for George to be in our business and be stressing over the shit we had going on so I slipped in the hallway bathroom to call Karter back just trying to check the temperature. I didn't know how to tell LeLe that I really didn't want shit bad to happen to Kim without offending her. Truth was, I still had love for Kim and I know somewhere deep inside LeLe did as well. It's just she was hurt beyond repair and I understood that whole-heartedly. "I missed your call Karter, what's up?" I quizzed leaning up against the bathroom counter.

"Hey beautiful. I was wondering if you've heard from Kim. Emily says she fled to Miami for whatever reason and we haven't heard from her all day. She won't even pick up her phone."

"I heard she's here but I haven't seen her. I mean, Karter you knew this day was coming. She had to come home and make it right. You do realize that Miami is home for her? Kim knows these streets better than the curves on her body. I'm sure she's fine. Let her handle her business."

"Oh I'm not worried." She sassed. "It's Emily who's obsessing over Kim and her entire situation."

I furrowed my brows at the tone in her voice. "Am I sensing a twinge of jealousy?" I asked knowing damn well she better not have been jealous over no damn Kim. If she was jealous than maybe Kim had indeed changed.

Karter sucked her teeth. "No way. I would never. She's still my sister. All I'm saying is Emily has committed herself to the well-being of Kim and Junior."

"Well, has she changed?" I asked.

"To be honest, I think she has. I just don't want to speak too soon. Whatever she has going on I'll pray for her. I hope she's fine. I'll let Emily know as well. I'll talk to you later Queen." She said before hanging up. She didn't even give me the chance to ask about Barbie or nothing. Karter wanted that baby all to herself. When I walked out of the bathroom I ran smack into Trell and LeLe in the living room. LeLe looked as if she was reading his ass to the filth, but when they saw me the conversation stopped.

I sucked my teeth and shook my damn head before walking up to Trell. I used my pointer finger and mushed him right in the middle of his forehead. "Oh you showing yo entire ass already ain't you? This is sad Trell. This isn't a good way to start off at all."

"What I tell you bout putting yo hands on me." He frowned looking as if something else were on his mind. "I wasn't with a bitch, cause I know that's what you thought. My bad for not calling but I had a lot going on."

LeLe just looked back and forth before excusing herself.

"Let me talk to you outside." I suggested so we could get a little more privacy. When I got him on the porch I continued. "Trell, do you remember that conversation that I had with you about relationships and how niggas be thinking that's what they want, but people don't really want to put in the…"

He cut me off. "Yeah, yeah, the blood, sweat, and tears and shit that come with it. I already know this ma. That aint the case aiight? I had to make a money move that will leave me straight for a lil bit. That's the God honest truth and that's probably telling you too much."

I shook my head. "This street shit ain't where it's at Trell. You have dreams and goals."

"Yeah, and I don't want that kind of shit around me either Trell!" LeLe yelled from the inside. We ignored her and walked further into the driveway after realizing she was listening. I knew Trell, and I knew something else was bothering him as well.

"What's really going on?"

He wiped his hand down his fine ass face. "I just got a lot of shit on my mind."

"You shouldn't even have any worries though. All your dreams are about to come true bae."

He shook his head. "No the fuck they not. A nigga ain't gettin' drafted Abbey." He said looking defeated. "That's some shit I haven't even told my family yet so I'mma need you to respect that."

I immediately felt bad for him. "Awww baby, it's gonna be okay. You can do anything. You have a degree, you're smart as hell, and outside of that thug shit you one of the smartest men I know Trell."

"Yeah ma, but you don't know what that shit feel like when you got the weight of the world on yo shoulders tryna make sure everybody straight. I gotta figure some shit out."

"It'll work itself out." I assured him hoping that I was some kind of comfort. I thought about doing something nice for him like cooking again, but I would definitely have to cook him the same damn thing I made last time cause that's the only dish I'd perfected and it took me forever to do that. I couldn't cook shit else to save my life. Trell didn't reply, he looked as though he was in deep thought before giving me his undivided attention. "I can make some phone calls for you." I told him since his degree was physical therapy in sports.

"Listen shorty, it's a nice gesture but ion need yo help with that. I'm my own man. I can find my own damn job." He chuckled giving me that look he gave me when he wanted some pussy. "When you goin' home?" He asked looking at me with his head tilt to the side.

I held my hand out up against his chest. "After the shit you pulled. You ain't off the hook that easy. I'm not one of these young ass hoes who's just happy to have some dick." I shook my head. "Nope... not me." I made sure I put an extra 'pop' on the P. "I have some errands to run first." I kissed his cheek walking to my car. Tell LeLe I'll call her.

Trell gave me a disapproving look but he watched me back out and leave until I was no longer in his eye view. As soon as I got home I showered, rolled me a joint, and poured me a glass of wine before sitting out on the porch with my short house dress on watching the way the Miami streets lit up as my eyes focused on all of the cars flying by. The night air felt so damn good kissing my peach smelling skin.

The way the weed had me feeling was at an all time high. I was on a cloud I had no intention on coming down off of. I knew I was gonna get some good sleep tonight. Briefly, Kim ran across my mind. I couldn't help but to wonder what the hell Majestic was doing to that girl right now. I wondered if he even let her live at all. I couldn't lie and say I wouldn't be sad. I could only pray for her. I'd call him tomorrow and see if I could get him to meet me somewhere to reconsider things. That baby deserved a mother.

Just as I was getting ready to go inside, Trell was pulling up and hopping out. He smelled just like I liked. A perfect mixture of cologne and weed. He wore a pair of basketball shorts, some Gucci slides, and a white tee with his chain dangling from around his neck. "What you doin' here?" I slowly licked my lips lusting over him.

Trell didn't say one word to me, instead, he lift me from the chair and carried me inside of the house making sure to lock the door behind him. There wasn't any words between us. Just like any other time, we were like magnets on each other, but I had to crush his goals of getting some pussy. "My period is still on Trell." I told him in between kisses as I pushed him down on the couch while hungrily pulling his hard, throbbing dick from his boxers under his basketball shorts.

"Ion wanna hear that nasty ass shit ma, just get me right." He told me giving me a serious look. The way Trell stared at me made me feel as though he was trying to dig into my soul. Like he was trying to read the most intimate parts of me and at times it scared the shit out of me. At the same time, I think this was a feeling that any woman would love to feel. My mouth watered looking at his juicy dick.

The smell of men's dove body wash tickled my nostrils, which was a plus. Trust me, I loved the smell of a clean dick. It was the niggas whose balls smelled like onions that got on my fucking nerves, and those the one always wanted a bitch to put their mouth on they stank ass.

Gently spitting over the tip. I opened my warm, wet mouth and slowly went down making sure to gently suck on my way up. One hand gripped his dick and the other hand worked his balls. I used my hands massaging both as I went to work on his ass making him remember why he chose me. Those lil young girls ain't know what the hell they were doing anyway.

Trell placed his hand on the back of my head and slowly guided me up and down. Ironically it turned me on even more while he expressed how good I was making him feel. When I felt his shit throbbing I knew he was about to cum. I held my tongue over his thick vein and worked it up and down until he was exploding in my mouth. Looking up at him, I licked my lips and let a little of his cum trickle down the side of my mouth before I stood up and walked away.

When I returned, Trell was staring at me. "You lucky yo period on ma. That's all imma say cause I would've been punishing that pussy in the worst way. When that shit goin' off anyway?"

I shrugged. "Soon playboy... soon."

"Good." He licked his full lips watching me clean him up. "I'mma make sure I got hella plan B's on deck cause I definitely gotta get me some of that." He kissed my forehead and pulled me on the couch with him. "You cooked?"

I snuggled up on his chest and sucked my teeth. "Hell no. You know my ass can't cook." I giggled. "I can order you some wings though."

"Now that we a couple, you gone have to learn how to cook ma. I know you don't want none of them young hoes feedin' me." He replied. I knew he was joking but still, I didn't wanna have to fuck this man up.

"Yeah, okay. Play if you want and watch how I find me a sugar daddy to chew this ass."

"Abbey… man…"

I cut him off laughing hard as hell. "I'm joking. I'm joking."

"Yeah, aiight." He grabbed the remote and turned on Netflix. I ended up ordering us some wings and fries so we munched that shit down when it came and then smoked a joint together before drinking a glass of Remy. When it was all said and done me and Trell passed out on the couch and I felt so good being in his arms. I really wanted to completely open up my heart to him, but LeLe's words always played in my head and I just had to make sure he wasn't about to try to have me out here playing the fool. His shit better had been cleaned up. I hated for people to be able to tell me 'I told you so'.

Chapter 4

Latrell 'Trell' Wells

Looking into Abbey's sleeping face, I needed her to understand there was no other place I'd rather be than right here where I was. She had no idea how hard it was to just cut everybody off, and that didn't mean just cause a nigga tried to cut all ties with everybody that was gone be all good. It was females who felt like they had just as much time with me as she did, what they failed to realize was they didn't have my heart. I ignored calls all day cause it was true, I needed to focus, but at the same time, I had a few bitches mad with me and wanted some answers as in to why they got cut the fuck off.

The only one I couldn't bring myself to hurt in that way was Liyah cause she had been real cool, and I cared about the girl but her obsession with a nigga wasn't even funny. She just didn't get it, no matter how much I ignored her. She wanted me to spend her birthday with her today, but I had shit to do and cause of my thing with Abbey, I couldn't do it anyway. In reality, Abbey was the only female who even gave me a run for my money or knew how to handle me the least bit. Where other females let me do what I wanted, Abbey wasn't for that shit and she was very vocal about it. I couldn't do shit but respect that.

In the wee hours of the morning there was a knock on Abbey's door. Since she was probably half tipsy and high, she didn't even hear her door, but since I was a light sleeper, I did. In my mind, I assumed it was one of her niggas who didn't easily take rejection. I got up slowly making sure not to wake her up and then grabbed my gun off of the table. I had already been a lil paranoid these past few days feeling like a nigga was being followed. I was constantly over my shoulder and that's why I was extra careful when I drove to Tampa to bust that lick. I was in and out.

I checked the peephole, but I didn't see anybody so I slowly unlocked the door and eased my way out. I thought my eyes was playing tricks on me when I saw Liyah posted up against my car waiting for me to come out. Looking back over my shoulder, I made sure Abbey was still sleep before I walked out to check her lil ass. I instantly saw 'red' cause a nigga didn't even play like this. Under no circumstance was it ever okay for any bitch to think she could disrespect me or my girl. If she wanted to holla at me face-to-face that's one thing, but she could've did that shit at my crib.

I didn't even give her chance to say shit before I was yoking her ass up by the shirt lifting her from the ground. Her feet were dangling underneath her and I saw the fear in her eyes. I didn't even hit females, but no bitch was gonna try me like this. "You the one been fuckin' following me?! The fuck you doin' at this girl muthafuckin' house!?" I barked. "You done lost yo fuckin' mind."

Liyah scratched at my hands trying to get me to let her down but I didn't give a fuck, and when I saw the tears falling it made me even angrier. I didn't wanna do this girl like this, at the same time I didn't know she was on some stalker type shit either. "Why you doing me like this Trell?" She asked with her voice cracking. "Why I gotta follow you to find out what it really is? I thought she was like a sister to you. You fucking her?" She questioned. I didn't owe her any explanation.

"I don't owe you shit Liyah. You ain't my fuckin' wife. You wasn't even my girl. We was kickin' it and that shit dead now. Don't you ever in yo life pull no shit like this." I growled before letting her go. "I guarantee you don't even want them kinda problems with me and I mean that shit. Take yo muhfuckin' ass on." I warned.

"You better." Abbey's voice boomed from the doorway sounding calm. Fuck, I didn't want her to wake up and see this shit and start thinking I was on some bullshit cause I wasn't. "If you don't want me beating your ass, I promise you better not ever show up to my house again." She was leaned up against the doorframe with both her arms crossed in front of her chest with some bedroom slippers on her feet.

"I got this, Abbey. Go back inside." I told her.

"Ha! Not in a million years. Not at my fucking house while some bitch out here tryna check you. See what happens when you bring hoes that's not even yo real girl around ya family? They start thinking they're entitled and shit." She pointed at me. "It's you niggas faults."

I just shook my muthafuckin' head and clutched my jaws cause she was really starting to piss me off. I didn't need her mouth too. Abbey definitely wanted me to grab her by that skinny ass duck neck of hers. "Listen ma, I get it aiight. I got it."

"I don't know what you want with that old bitch anyway." Liyah grilled me.

"Girl please, I'm barely three years older than the nigga. Don't hate cause he chose a pussy that's a lil more seasoned. Now get yo young ass outta here before you catch splinters in ya ass waiting on a nigga." Abbey barked. She was way too calm for me but I know her words cut deep cause if I was a female that shit would've definitely done something to my ego.

I guess she decided that she had no more words for Liyah, cause she walked back inside of the house on her own. I looked back to Liyah. "You gonna let her talk to me like that? You like females who talks like that? She's a fucking gutter rat." She frowned.

I warned her for the last time. "Get yo simple ass outta here Liyah. That's the last time I'mma tell you."

I guess she knew her time was running short because without another word, she walked away and hopped in her car. She stared at me with tears in her eyes before pulling off. I was hoping Abbey wasn't on the bullshit when I walked inside but there she was sitting on the couch heated. "Look, I'm sorry about that ma. You know I'd never disrespect you like that under no circumstance."

"Strike two Trell. Strike muthafuckin' two." She said hopping up. "I'm so damn mad I gotta go take me a shower to cool off."

I wasn't used to going through no shit like this and had it been any other female I wouldn't have given a fuck about her being mad at me. My motto was 'she'll get over it'. At the same time, nobody hardly ever questioned shit I did cause they just wanted to be in my presence. Abbey was right though, this relationship shit was different. I felt like I had to actually kiss ass to make things right and that's not something I was used to doing. I didn't know how to be this soft ass nigga. All I could do was try.

When I heard the shower water running. I walked into the bathroom where Abbey was showering. As soon as I opened the door the scent of peaches in the steam filled room hit my nose. Abbey didn't even realize I was standing here, but I didn't wanna get too close cause I didn't wanna see no blood and shit. My stomach couldn't take that. I wanted to say something. I just didn't know what to say. I just felt bad that dumb ass girl came over here. No matter what, no female deserved that.

I thought about doing something nice to make up with her so I walked in the kitchen to check her fridge to see what she had in there. Unlike Abbey, I could actually cook cause my mama didn't play that shit. I knew she had to be to work in a couple of hours, which meant she probably wasn't going back to sleep, so I took this time to make her a breakfast. I was surprised she even kept groceries, wasn't like she could actually cook any of this shit, she could only try.

I took out some eggs, maple bacon, and made some Aunt Jemima pancake mix to make some banana pancakes. The smell instantly lit up the house when I started. By the time Abbey finally came out from getting dressed in her work clothes, I was halfway done. "What you in here doing?" She gave me a half smile sitting at the table.

"Cookin' you breakfast before you go to work. It's the least I could do." I told her scrambling up the eggs. When I was done, I put everything on the plate and sat it down in front of her. I melted some butter next and poured it on top of her pancakes before putting the syrup. "You want me to cut the shit up too?" I asked her being funny.

She chuckled. A nigga was just glad she was smiling. She had to know that shit wasn't on me. "Boy, you don't gotta cut my damn pancakes. I'm grown."

"I'm just sayin'." I shrugged. "I ain't never in my life cooked for a female outside of my mama and my sister. That's on everything."

"So is this some kind of apology?" She asked popping a piece of bacon in her mouth.

I sat across from her. "I'm tryin'."

"Well this was a good gesture."

I stared at her pretty freckled face for a few seconds wondering what was really on her mind. "Does our age difference bother you? Keep it real."

She stopped chewing like she was thinking about it. She shrugged. "Not really. If it did, I wouldn't have agreed to be with you. I'm just not beat for your hoes throwing it up in my face. I'm about to be twenty-six in a few weeks. One would think I was some kinda old hag."

"Nah, you ain't that at all. You beautiful as fuck. Far from an old hag."

A wide smile spread across her face. "Let me find out you're trying to be sweet."

I stood up from the table and chuckled. "Yep, that's my cue to head on out." I had some shit to do and I needed to holla at Majestic. "Today is LeLe's birthday. She tell you about any plans?"

"She's my best friend Trell. Of course I know it's her birthday, but I don't know what she wants to do. I'll call her when I get off." She told me. Abbey ate everything on her plate and then went to the sink to wash the plate out. After brushing her teeth again and grabbing her purse and keys, we walked out together. She kissed me on the cheek before getting in her car assuring me that she would call me on her lunch break. I returned to my own car and drove in the opposite direction so I could go to Majestic's house since the trap was shut down.

When I pulled up to Majestic's house, it was odd hearing a crying baby on the other side of the door. I assumed this nigga done went and got him a bitch and playing the step daddy role. "Who is it?" He asked.

"Nigga, you know who it is. You want this bread or not?" I asked.

The door unlocked and he let me and my duffle bag inside of the house. I was surprised to see he was actually holding a baby. A little ass baby. A newborn. "Sup." He spoke and then locked the door.

"Nigga, who baby is this? I know damn well nobody wasn't crazy enough to have yo ass baby sitting." I frowned confused. My eyes quickly bounced around the house. This nigga had baby swings, playpens, bouncers and all that baby shit. Shit looked like daddy's daycare. I don't know when he was able to get all this shit. I had only been gone for a day and a half. He looked like he was handling it though. He picked the half empty bottle off of the table and sat down so he can feed him.

"Shhh, daddy got you." He said trying to console the baby.

I raised a brow. "Daddy?"

"Yeah nigga. Daddy. This my son. Majestic Jr." He said all proud like and shit.

Now I wasn't the one to try to rain on his parade, but I had never heard this nigga say he had a baby on the way. I'd never seen no bitch that he fucked with for that matter. "Whoa, slow down killa. Now I'm happy for you and all but I ain't never heard you say shit about no baby. Did Dana confirm that?" I asked him referring to a DNA. I swore on everything I loved that unless a female gave me a DNA test, I wasn't claiming anything. These females ain't play fair. They played more games than the NBA. Hell, they could teach us a thing or two.

Majestic turned the baby around so I could get a better look. "Nigga, he's mine. I don't need a DNA to see that, clearly. But I did one anyway and sent that shit in the mail today."

I nod my head. "Who the mama?"

He sighed and wiped his hand down his face. "It's complicated."

I heard a noise coming from the back. Sounded like somebody was knocking on the wall. "Who the fuck is that? You aint tell me you had somebody here. I'm glad I didn't start counting this bread."

"Nah, it ain't like that." He said standing up walking to the back. I sat and watched until he disappeared. This shit was getting weird as fuck but I didn't have any more time to waste so I started counting out his half of the money so I could leave. When he came back, he didn't have the baby. At this point, I wasn't even asking no questions cause it wasn't none of my muhfuckin' business. We handled our business and I bounced. No need in me getting in his business. If he wanted me to know something, he would've told me.

Chapter 5

Leandra 'LeLe' Wells

"Happy birthday to you. Happy birthday to you. Happy birthday dear LeLeeeee. Happy birthday to you!" My team at McDonald's sang to me surprising me with a big ass cake after my shift. I really tried to smile, but it was so damn hard. I had made myself very clear with everybody that I didn't want shit done for me. This day was always bittersweet. What bothered me the most is being twenty-five years in age and not being where I wanted to be. I was supposed to be well off into my career by now, but here I was still trying to figure it out all cause of a simple bitch.

Still, I didn't wanna seem ungrateful so I made sure to thank them and then I sliced everybody up a piece of cake and passed it out before grabbing my things and heading to my car feeling sad as fuck. I slung my purse in the passenger seat and rest my head on the headrest. If I could crawl under a rock for the rest of the day and disappear, I would. I promised myself that I wouldn't cry. On this day 3 years ago, I got engaged. I lost the love of my life. I lost my child. I lost my life. There was no way I could be happy with Malik laying in the grave. People just wouldn't understand.

After I got myself together, I pulled off and drove to the drive-thru store to get me a strawberry big dipper before getting home. When I arrived, I walked inside not wanting to be bothered but I had a huge flower arrangement that was waiting for me on the table. I dropped my keys on the counter. "Maaa! Who did this come from?" I yelled to the back while checking for a note or something.

She walked from the back eating a granola bar. "I don't know LeLe but stop yelling cause George is sleeping. He hasn't been feeling too well today." She shrugged and stood next to me admiring the flowers. "All I did was sign for them when they showed up, they're pretty though."

I passed them to her. "Well you can have them if you want."

"These are your birthday flowers, especially for you LeLe." She tried to decline.

I practically shoved them in her face. I didn't even know whom they came from because there wasn't a note. "You know I'm just gonna let them die anyway. I've never been good with flowers. You know this."

She took them with no problem after that and then went to place them in a flower vase filled with water. Then she added a little sugar to the water and sat the vase on the table. "I sho will take care of these." She smiled at them and then looked at me. "By the way, if the house phone rings, answer it. I'm trying to see about getting a job."

"A job?" I frowned. "Who's gonna look after George if you get a job? Why you want a job anyway? Trell pays all the bills and so do I."

"I don't wanna put that kind of pressure on either one of you. Especially Trell. I'm just waiting on him to tell me he's not getting drafted since I already heard the news anyway."

"Whattt?" I frowned. "How you know?"

"I'm his mama. It's certain shit I should know. Certain shit I'm supposed to know. Just like I knew him and Leon was out there selling them drugs too."

I just looked at her.

"Umhmm don't look at me crazy. I keep telling ya'll I wasn't born yesterday." She replied as she walked away to go back to the back room. I was so damn tired that I went to the room and fell on the bed face first with my work clothes still on. I felt like I hadn't rest in days. Next time I woke up, it was well into the night. I checked my phone to multiple missed calls from everybody. Kevin sent me a text asking if I liked my flowers. That explained where those came from. I couldn't even be mad with him cause he didn't know any better.

I called Trey back since I had one missed call from him. When he answered, it sounded like he had a lot of noise in the background, which was unusual. "What up birthday girl." He spoke causing me to raise a brow. I hadn't told him it was my birthday at all.

"How do you know it's my birthday? I didn't tell you that." I yawned rubbing the sleep from my eyes.

"Cause I'm supposed to know. You in for the night?"

"I mean, not if I don't have to be."

"Aiight, I'mma come grab you." He said before hanging up. He never waited for me to reply. He just always told me what he wanted or expected of me and my job was to make it happen. I hopped up and went to take me a shower. When I was done, I took my long hair and part it down the middle before slicking me a ponytail to the back allowing my hair to hang. I took a little edge brush and applied my cute baby hairs before getting dressed. I wanted to be comfortable so I put on a pair of Ethika tights with the matching top and my Nike Airmax. I grabbed the matching jacket just in case it got cold. I applied just a little eyeliner around my eyes and put on some nude lip-gloss. In reality, I didn't feel like going anywhere, but to be next to Trey and all in his business, I would go.

Within thirty minutes he was calling me telling me to come outside. As soon as I hopped in, his YSL tickled my nose. Trey looked like he had a fresh tape around the edges. He wore a simple gold chain that had a cross dangling from it and no other jewelry. He was dressed down in Armani Exchange. "Hey Trey."

Trey looked at me briefly. "Where yo clothes at?"

I shrugged. "I'm wearing them. I'm fully covered. Don't start." I giggled.

"How was your day shorty?"

"I worked and that was it. I don't like doing much on this day, too many bad memories. It's just another day. Nothing special. But listen, I hope everything goes well with that inspection. My mama just laid some news on me that I didn't agree with. I have to move fast."

He focused on the road. "I mean I think it should be cool. It's a cool lil spot."

"Why don't you ever go in detail when it comes to certain things?"

"What you mean ma?"

"Meaning, why didn't you ask me what happened with my mama."

"Listen, I assume if you wanted me to know you would've told me. I'm not big on meddling in people's business like that."

"You meddled when you didn't want me around Cass." I shrugged.

He looked at me before responding, and then back to the road. "That was different. I was tryna keep yo hardheaded ass outta trouble and from going back to some shit that wasn't built for you. You can't even compare the two. That's like comparing apples to grapes. It ain't no comparison."

I nod my head. "I get it. Where are we going?"

Instead of answering me, he reached in the backseat and grabbed a tiny Pandora bag and handed it to me. "Here you go."

I sat the bag in my lap and stared. "You didn't have to get me anything Trey. I mean, it's a nice gesture and all but I don't really like gifts or celebrations on this day. I'm sure you understand."

"I do. It ain't like that though. Just open it."

I did as I was told. It was an Pandora necklace that had a single charm hanging from it symbolizing inner strength. It was beautiful. "Aww. I love this so much. Thanks Trey. I really appreciate this."

"Ain't much, but I'm glad you like it." He told me pulling up to 'Da Nolia'. Everybody knew that these were some of the roughest projects in Miami. There were kids running around the fire hydrants in the dark. There was niggas gambling on the stoops. Females braiding hair on the stoops. It was a very strong smell of alcohol, fried chicken, and piss when he opened the door to get out. "I'll be right back." He told me. I watched him walk up the steps and disappear into the building. I sat for a few minutes and waited for him. He didn't take long. He came right back out.

"Who lives here?" I asked.

"My uncle and my aunt Sue." He replied and pulled off. "You got plans? You gotta be home soon?"

"No."

"Cool."

Chapter 6

Leandra 'LeLe' Wells

Trey rode in silence for the next fifteen minutes before we were pulling up to a big pretty ass house. The landscaping was perfect. The Palm Trees out front; I could tell were planted there. The driveway was full of luxury cars and regular ones as well but mostly luxury. I wondered if a bunch of dope boys owned these cars. "Come on." Trey told me when he turned the ignition off. I stepped out of the truck looking around. "I ain't gone let nothin' happen to you shorty." He came around to my side and placed his hand inside of mine. "You trust me?"

I looked down at my hand in his. This is was the first real physical sign of affection that Trey had ever shown me. I nod my head. "Yeah, I trust you." I told him. Ironically, I trusted him even when I barely even knew him. I just never listened to him because of my own feelings.

"Good, you wit' me now. This my peoples house and my family is yo family so relax." He told me walking me to the side gate that led into the backyard. I was so into Trey's ass. I could honestly say he was way different than any other nigga I'd met. He reminded me a lot of Malik. He was never doing too much, low key, wasn't on no clown shit and genuinely cared about me.

I tried hard to ignore the butterflies in my stomach. That feeling that you got when you met a new nigga and it was fresh and early on. When we finally made it to the back of the house, it was an entire backyard party. They had a DJ and all and it was full of people I didn't know. I recognized one face. A girl named Bari who we went to high school with. She was one of those quiet girls though.

She never hung with nobody besides a girl named Bambi. We didn't personally know each other, but we were cordial whenever passing in the hallways and shit. She was still pretty and looked like she'd put on some pounds cause she was skinny as hell back then. It looked good on her. She was like a slim-thick now.

We locked eyes and she waved at me with a smile. I waved back and leaned into Trey. "Whose house did you say this was again? I know her." I spoke of Bari.

He followed my eyes to her. "Oh, that's my lil cousin Bari. This her brother house, Gu and his wife Qui." He told me.

The DJ yelled over the MIC. "Cool ass Trey! What up nigga?" He saluted him placing all eyes on us.

Trey looked his way and saluted him back as he spoke before making his rounds. There was a table full of buffet styled food and it smelled good too. It was a few different flavors of ribs, mac and cheese, baked beans, potato salad and more. It smelled so good. There was a built in bar by the pool area and two pretty chicks was behind the bar mixing drinks and getting tipped well while they were at it. Trey led me to a dude on the grill that looked exactly like him. It was so fucking scary. The resemblance was undeniable. "Assalamualaikum cuz." Trey greeted the dude slapping hands with him. Like Trey, he had those thick eyebrows, full lashes, and full lips. His skin was as dark as Godiva chocolate like Trey's and he wore his hair with dreads. His tapeline was crispy too. Trey and him were the same exact height. I was convinced they had to be brothers.

"Mualaikumsalam cuz." The dude greeted me back. He took a swig from the Remy bottle he was holding. He wore a simple white wife beater tee. A pair of Robin Jeans and some fresh ass J's on his feet. Around his neck he wore a huge medallion and he smelled good too. I peeped the ring on his wedding finger. He was married. "How you doin' ma?" He reached out to shake my hand. "I'm Gu." He said with the same calmness that Trey always showed. This nigga was too cool for me.

"Hi." I smiled. "I'm LeLe."

"Nice to meet you ma. You want a drink?" He asked.

"I don't drink. I'll take a water though."

"I can respect that. You want some food? Shit we got plenty of it. Granna and wifey threw down."

My eyes bounced around trying to see which one may have been the one they called Granna. I didn't see anyone who would be old enough to call Granna. "I'll eat in a few. Thank you." I smiled. I needed to get away from him. This nigga was too damn fine.

"Messiah Carter!" An older lady came walking over. Her skin was just as dark as theirs and she was beautiful as hell with a head full of good curly hair. "Didn't I tell you we were gone run outta burgers fucking with these greedy niggas. Hell, when it's gone, it's gone." She threw her arms in the air and then brought them down wiping them on the front of her apron.

"Fuck that shit Sue. I'm not buying shit else. Fuck it." He shrugged.

She slapped Gu on his arm. "I'm ya mama. Stop calling me Sue! Been telling yo ass that for years." She then acknowledged Trey. "Hey nephew. Looking good."

He embraced her back. "Sup auntie." He then introduced us. "This LeLe. LeLe this my aunt Sue."

She looked me up and down before speaking. She yelled over her shoulder. "Ma! Becka! Get on over here!" She said just like the aunt who always got drunk at the family parties. A few seconds later another woman who looked just like his aunt Sue and then an older woman who looked just like them both came walking up together. "Becka, this is LeLe." She said. "LeLe this my sister Becka. This is our mama, her name is Granna. Ma…" She chuckled. "She came with Trey."

"Nah auntie, ya'll ain't bout to embarrass a nigga." Trey told them giving Becka and Granna a hug. He then looked to Gu. "Let me holla at you real quick."

Gu and Trey walked away but not before Gu spoke his mind to Sue. "Back up ma, give the girl some breathin' room. Ya'll gone scare the girl away lookin' at her like a T-bone steak and shit." He shook his head.

"Boy. You better watch your damn sour ass mouth." Granna scolded him. She smiled at me. "How you doing young lady? Are you Trey's girlfriend?"

"Gotta be his girlfriend cause that boy ain't ever brought no female around us." Becka replied for me.

Sue lightly slapped her sister's arm. "Shut up and let the girl talk Becka, damn."

I don't know why I felt like I was getting interrogated but I liked their crazy asses. I didn't know how to reply besides tell the truth. "No... we're just..."

Bari walked up cutting me off. "What friends?" She giggled. "Girl please. Whether you know it or not you're his damn girl. He would never bring nobody around here otherwise so what did you do?"

I raised a brow. "Huh?"

She shrugged. "What did you do? Cause you must have some kryptonite in that pus-..."

Granna cut her off. "Hey! I wish you would Bari! You're not too old to get your little ass beat." She warned.

"Mama don't threaten my child. The girl is grown." Sue chuckled.

"My bad Granna." Bari mumbled. "Um you wanna walk over here with me?" Bari grabbed my hand leading me away from the old folks. "We'll be back ya'll." She lied and then said to me. "I had to get you away from their ass or you would've been stuck over there all night."

I laughed. "Appreciate that cause girl I didn't know what the hell to say. Omg how you been Bari? It's been a long ass time girl. You look good."

"I've been okay girl." She stopped in front of the food. "I'm hungry as hell. You better eat before these niggas eat it all up." She grabbed two plates. "Qui! Ya'll fixing plates or you want us to do it?"

The chick came over to us instead of yelling from the sliding back door where she was standing. She was brown skin and real pretty and exotic looking. She had a couple of tattoos but the one that stood out the most was the half sleeve on her arm. It was so pretty. She had huge brown eyes and wore her hair on some faux locs. "Hell no, I'm not a maid. I done cooked and I'm tired as hell. I'm aggravated as fuck too." She furrowed her brows. "Girl if Gu don't control his baby mama I'mma kill her."

Bari laughed. "You and Nessy have this 'love, hate' type of relationship. You know she's crazy as hell."

"Yeah okay." She mumbled under her breath rolling her eyes.

Bari introduced us. "This is LeLe and she came with Trey. She's Trey's girl."

"I'm not." I told her. "But nice to meet you."

She gave me a side way look. "Girl, if that nigga got you here. You're definitely is girl, even if you don't know it yet. Anyway..." She extended her hand. "Nice to meet you. I'm Gu's wife, my name is Qui."

I didn't know why everybody kept saying that shit like be being around was so shocking. Maybe it was, hell I didn't know. I was still trying to learn about Trey. He had never even taken me to his place. Just as hard as it was for women to trust men. It was just as hard for Trey to trust anybody, it didn't matter who it was. "Nice to meet you too." I told her.

After we fixed plates. I walked off to sit down under one of the table umbrellas and ate my food while scrolling my phone and listening to the music the DJ was playing. Trey and Gu kept disappearing but he would come to me occasionally to ask if I was okay. "You good shorty?" He asked for the third time sitting directly across from me. I nod my head telling him 'yes'. "I forgot to tell you not to forget your plate. I fixed it and had Gu's wife put it up for me."

"Good lookin'." He replied. "I like that. You enjoying yo'self?"

"For the most part." I told him. "What's the occasion though?"

"It's Becka's birthday."

"Ohhh." I replied. "I didn't know that. You should've told me so I could've at least told her happy birthday."

"It ain't too late. You'll see here again before the night is over with." He told me. I guess he sensed the look on my face. "Wussup shorty? Speak ya mind. You ain't gotta ever hold back from sayin' shit to me."

"It's just..." I sighed. "I'm having fun. I don't want you to think I'm not having fun. I'm just wondering why you brought me here?"

He did something that I didn't expect. For the second time tonight, he placed his hands in mine. "You wanna get to know me right? What better way than to bring you around the people I love the most."

"Word?" I giggled.

"You see my cousin Gu? He's the realest nigga I know and he's solidified in these streets. I trust that nigga with my life ma. He's a pretty good judge of character too and ain't nothin' that nigga ain't been through. Had he said anything flaky about you, I would've cut this shit short right now. You see Bari and Qui? Granna and Becka? Even Sue's crazy ass? They all been through some shit but I'm not even finna go into all of that. They story so lit, they had to write a book about they ass. Hard Lovin' Straight Thuggin' you can check it out cause ion have time to sit here and tell it all. Back to what I was saying though, if they would've told me something ain't right about you, this shit would be dead right now. Not one of them told me that got a bad vibe, that means a lot."

I raised a brow. "So did you bring me here to meet everybody and learn more about you? Or did you bring me here to be studied?" I asked.

"Both."

"So what was I supposed to learn about you?"

"Shit, what's the most you heard about me all night?" He asked.

I chuckled. "Obviously you don't bring no bitches around them and they keep saying I gotta be your girl if I'm here."

Trey gave me a serious look. "Aiight then shorty, act like you know. I'm not really here to play no games LeLe. I've been studying you since I met you. You think a nigga put his freedom on the line for nothing? I've been rooting from you since day one. Ain't too many sold females out here."

Lord, Trey was laying it on me real thick. Of course I wanted him to open up to me more and I was really liking this side of him. I just didn't know what to say. "So you want me to be your girl?"

He gave me a look he never gave me before. It was that look as if to say he would definitely put it on my ass. My pussy instantly started jumping. It had jumped a few times tonight. I would be lying if I said I didn't wanna pursue something more with Trey, I just didn't wanna put myself completely out there like that. "We gone do this or we ain't ma? When I want something, I don't mind going after it and doing whatever to make sure you straight by pushing you to the best of yo abilities. If this ain't what you want I need to know now."

Thoughts of Malik clouded my mind. I knew this was a part of the healing process. I had to move on. "Yes Trey… slowly, but yes." I smiled reaching across the table to place a kiss on his soft ass lips. I wasn't expecting to do that, and I didn't know how he would take it, but he embraced it. Like sugar, I melted to his touch. We were so engulfed in our moment that we didn't even realize someone was walking up.

"Awe mayne get a fuckin' room with allat." I looked up and a cute ass light skin dude with light eyes and a lot of tattoos were standing over us. He looked familiar, real familiar.

"What up Pete?" Trey clapped him up and he did the same.

"Shit, surprised yo Casper the Ghost ass came out." He told Trey.

Trey nod his head. "This LeLe. LeLe this Pete. Bari's fiancé."

Pete and me locked eyes. "Sup shorty." He spoke.

I gave him a light wave. He looked real familiar. I knew I'd seen him around somewhere but couldn't put my finger on it. He gave his attention back to Trey. "Shit, I just got here. I had to drop Major off with the baby sitter. You know when they have these parties they be on that 'no kids allowed' bullshit."

"Shit, I already know." Trey told him standing up. It was time to sing happy birthday to aunt Becka. The three of us walked over just in time cause they were lighting the candles. After it was over. Trey stuck around talking to Gu for a few more minutes before we left. On the ride home, I was tired as hell. I had to go to work in the morning but I was calling out so we can get the inspection done.

"Thanks for everything Trey." I told him placing my hand on top of his. "I enjoyed myself. I needed that."

"Ain't no problem ma. I got you. I'mma grab you tomorrow before inspection." He told me. There was an awkward silence between us as we just looked at each other. Trey reached over and kissed me again before telling me to go in the house. He made sure he watched me until I made it in safe. I had a much different attitude then when I first left the house. As long as I was out I was fine but the minute I got back inside and it was just these walls and me. I couldn't ignore what this day represented. I looked at my watch. It was fifteen minutes before midnight. *Thank God this day is almost over.'* I mumbled to myself before laying down with Trey on my mind.

Chapter 7

Kimberly 'Kim' Laws

Majestic had me hostage in his house for days feeling like a prisoner, cause that's what I was. He didn't let me talk to anybody, he wouldn't even allow me to go the bathroom without his permission and it was literally killing me. I sat on the bed with one of my wrist cuffed to the pole on the edge of the bed with tears coming down my face. By junior being so tiny, I believe that's the only reason that majestic was even keeping me alive. I knocked on the wall of the room with my free hand. Within' a few seconds, majestic appeared in the doorway. "What the fuck you want Kim?" He growled at me.

I sighed. On the outside I may have been calm to him, but on the inside, my stomach was in knots. "I have to use the bathroom Majestic." I told him.

He walked away to go check on the baby before coming back to me pulling the key from his pocket to release me. He had warned me multiple times that he would put a bullet in my head if I tried to scream or run away. Majestic looked at me with so much hatred in his eyes that I couldn't even blame him. I'd been sitting on the bed so long today that my legs were cramped up. It hurt like hell when I tried to stand. He followed me to the bathroom and stood at the door watching me like a hawk without saying a word.

I felt nasty, disgusting, and hopeless. I felt as though I'd done all of that for nothing. I wasn't the same person and I couldn't make them believe me. The only thing that kept me going was my baby. If I had to live like a prisoner in order to open my eyes and see him for another day, I truly would. He was my strength and my whole heart. I pulled my panties down and sat on the toilet feeling weak. I hadn't been allowed to take a bath nor a shower in days. It was till the point that I was starting to smell myself and if I could smell myself, I knew he could. Majestic wanted to humiliate me and it was working, but I was trying hard not to break.

"Can I please take a shower?" I asked. "Please. Don't act like you don't smell me." I said shaking my head using the tissue to wipe myself.

"Strip and hop in the shower. The only reason I'mma let you bathe is cause ion want no stank ass pussy smelling up my fuckin' house Kim." He grilled me using one hand to hold his nose. "You fucked up killing my brother, you don't even deserve to breathe right now."

I drop my eyes in defeat. I didn't wanna be forced to keep talking because my mouth was dry as hell and I was over dehydrated. I slowly got up and peeled my moisten panties off and then removed my bra right in front of him. I weakly turned the shower on and stepped inside letting the hot water cascade all over my body. Taking hot showers were so underrated. Because Majestic didn't give me a hand rag, I had to grab the piece of tiny soap that he had in there and use my hands trying my best to scrub all over my body. He only gave me about two minutes before he was rushing me out.

He allowed me to dry off with a clean towel that he found under his sink. "I don't have anything to put on." I told him with shivering lips. I was so cold... so, so cold. I wish he would let me eat a decent meal, or have a glass of cold water. He thought about it for a moment and grabbed me roughly by the wrist before forcing me to sit on the bed. Next, he got a pair of basketball shorts and a big oversized shirt from his drawer and allowed me to put it on. Since they both were way too big for me, I had to tie them up to get them to fit. He didn't give me any lotion or nothing to lotion my ashy body. I blankly stared at him when he took my wrist cuffing it back to the bed. "I'm not gonna run Majestic, damn."

"I don't give a fuck. You think a nigga pose to trust you? Just stop talkin' to me yo." He said without even looking at me. As soon as he finished, he had to leave me alone again cause the baby was crying. Although he was so near, he seemed so far. Majestic only let me deal with him when he was becoming unbearable for him. He hadn't left this house in days. I sat hopelessly on the bed listening to his faint cries. A few minutes later, Majestic came walking in the room and lay him on the bed to change his wet diaper and then he attempted to feed him. Even after that, my baby still wouldn't quite settle.

"What's wrong with him yo?" Majestic frowned.

"He smells me Majestic. I'm his mother." My heart broke in a million pieces not being able to hold him when I wanted to. I imagine this is what jail would be like if I had to do the time for the crime that I committed. LeLe had to be one strong ass female cause this was so hard and heartbreaking. My heart broke even more for her. I kept telling myself if this was my fate I'd have to deal with it. It didn't change the fact that it still hurt.

Majestic rocked him in his arms before he just gave up and gave him to me. I didn't know what he expected me to do with one hand, but I cuffed him like a football in my free arm allowing him to feel me and smell me. He immediately settled down. Majestic left for about fifteen minutes and came back. When he saw that Junior was sleeping, he took him back. My stomach did a mean growl and I know he heard it but he didn't give a fuck. He simply walked away. Again, my ego was shook. Being here was taking me back to a bad place. A place that I had prayed my way up out of. The fear of what he was doing to me would make me turn back into somebody I truly didn't wanna be.

My eyes bounced around his plush room scanning for my phone. I didn't see it anywhere and I assumed he must've turned it off. I knew that Emily or Karter had to be looking for me. I wondered if they'd even called around asking about me. I wondered if they cared enough to put out a missing persons report or something. I didn't know how long I had been sitting here this time, but I dozed off and woke up to the smell of food causing my mouth to water. Majestic walked in the room and un-cuffed me causing me to grab my sore wrist and rub it. "Come on." He told me leading me out the room and to the dining room table. He pointed to the chair. "Sit down." I did as I was told and then he took my wrist and locked me up again to the chair next to me.

I didn't say shit to him I had nothing to say to him, the more he did this to me it was making me hate him. He didn't have to do this. He could've just taken me out of my misery but I guess it was more entertaining to just humiliate me. He sat in front of me with a plate full of steak with grilled onions and potatoes. He wanted me to ask where mine was but I refused. Using his fork and knife, he cut into the medium well steak as I watched the juices ooze out before he devoured it into his mouth. I dropped my head ignoring my hunger and trying to ignore the smell. Majestic had his eyes trained on me, I could feel it.

When he was satisfied with his meal, he got up and placed his plate in the sink. Next, he made me a cold ham and cheese sandwich with a cup of water and placed it in front of me. I didn't give a shit that it was only a sandwich. I was just glad to have some food in front of me. I used my free hand and devoured the food before gulping down the tall glass of water. I wanted to ask for another glass but I didn't wanna push it. Majestic looked irritated just looking at me. He frowned his face and pulled out his phone right in front of me. "Yo, what the fuck you tryna do? I'm tired of lookin' at this bitch." He barked. I assumed he was talking to LeLe since she was the only person that knew I was here. I don't know what she said to him over the phone but within a few seconds, he hung up.

Frustrated, he released me and then led me back to the room where he locked me up again. I wondered briefly if I kicked him in the balls or something could I make a dash for it. I knew that would only happen if I had to worry about myself only but if I did that I was putting my baby's life in danger as well. How could I make a dash for it and leave him behind? That wasn't an option. Majestic made another phone call when he walked back out and I could hear him talking. "Yeah ma, I been busy for a few days. Yeah, I know. I'll explain. Nah, I can't but you can over here. Come now." He told her.

I didn't know what the fuck he had planned, but at this point. I guess I had to just wait. I was tired of waiting not knowing the unexpected but I already knew the rules. Don't say shit or he was gonna kill me. I was slowly falling into a deep depression.

Chapter 8

Majestic Jones

I paced back and forth waiting for my mama to get here. I thought it was about time that I introduced her to her grandson. It was time for Kim's ass to go. The more I was forced to look at her, the more I hated her ass. There was nothing in me that felt sorry for this bitch. There wasn't one thing or person I loved more than my brother. The love I had for that nigga ran deeper than the love I had for my own mama and I put that on everything. A part of me felt bad for my son too. A bigger part of me was torn only for him. I didn't give a fuck about shit else. I needed my mama to get the baby though cause I'd been locked up in this house for days babysitting Kim's ass and I had some moves I needed to make.

When she knocked on the door I let her in. She immediately walked in fussing. "Boy, how in the hell do you just go missing… you know better than that." Her eyes scanned the room and she stopped. "What the hell is all of this baby stuff? You babysitting? Who had a baby? Lordddd. Who trusted you to watch a baby?" She frowned noticing the sleeping baby in the bassinet. I had all this shit delivered the second day of them being here.

"Ma… he's mine. He's your grandson. Majestic Junior." I told her watching for her reaction but it wasn't what I expected.

She shook her head. "Boy, I raised you to be smarter than that. You haven't told me nothing about no baby and then you just show up with one? Did a trick try to pin a baby on you? Don't you let nobody just pin a baby on you. You's a damn fool. Did you take a test?"

"I did ma." I told her getting agitated. Maybe calling her right now wasn't a good idea. "I'm waiting for the results, but you're more than welcome to hold him. I called you over here to meet him but if you ain't tryna do that then you can go."

Her eyes started watering up and she piped down a little bit and softened up. "If he's not mine Majestic. I don't wanna sike myself up and get overly excited. You understand don't you?"

I sighed. "Mama, just look at him."

She slowly walked over to the bassinet and since he was sleeping on his back, she was able to get a real good look at him. She gasped bringing her hand up to her mouth. She looked from me to him, from him to me. She then went in her wallet and pulled out of baby picture of Malik and one of me placing it next to the baby's face. The tears overwhelmed her eyes. "Omg Majestic. He looks exactly like you and Malik. Awww shuga." She cried as she gently rubbed the baby's head. "Can I hold him?" She asked.

"Yeah ma, you gotta wash your hand first though." I told her.

"Right." She rushed away to the hall bathroom to wash her hands. I took Junior out of his bassinet and grabbed his blanket preparing for my mama to come hold him. About two minutes later, she came back out with a look of disapproval on her face. "Majestic, isn't that LeLe's friend Kim? I know her, I know that face. I remember her so don't you lie to be boy. She may be a little older than last time I saw her, but I don't forget a face."

I could've slapped myself for letting her take her nosey ass back there. "Yeah" I replied. "Here." I passed her the baby as she gently cuffed him in her arms still grilling me.

"Why the hell is she locked up to the damn bed Majestic? What kind of freak shit do ya'll have going on?" She asked.

"It ain't like that ma. Fuck Kim." I spat.

She raised a brow. "So was it true? What LeLe was trying to tell me?" She took a seat on the couch.

I wiped my bare hand down my face. "Yeah, all this time we been blaming LeLe ma. It ain't even her fault. This bitch been living her life. Ran off and had my baby. Made me miss out on his birth and all and then acts like everything pose to be all good."

My mama just stared at the baby instead of looking at me like she was in deep thought. "I said some mean stuff to LeLe. We are all hurting but you can't hold her hostage. You gotta let her go son."

"The fuck?" I frowned.

She said it again. "Let her go. Sometimes you have to just let go and let God. You can't hold her hostage. She bore your child. She's your son's mother."

"So I'm supposed to say fuck Malik cause this bitch had a baby?"

"Watch your goddamn mouth. You're getting a little too comfortable boy." She scolded me. "I'm not saying forget about it, none of us will ever forget about it. I'm saying let it go. Even if I don't want to forgive her, I have to because if it wasn't for her..." She looked at the baby again. "I wouldn't be holding him." She sighed. "Just let it go. I'm sure she's been through a lot or even been beating her own self up."

"She's just a fucked up person."

"Looking into that girl's eyes... I don't think so son. The strength she's in there trying to display is truly the strength of a mother and you will never understand."

I didn't wanna hear no more of what she had to say. "You wanna take him for the night? I have some stuff to do."

Her eyes lit up. "Yeah, does he have everything? I'd love to take him." She cooed wearing a happiness in her eyes that I hadn't seen in a long time. "I'm kind of nervous." She chuckled. "It's been so long."

"I'm sure you'll be aiight." I assured her.

When I made sure she had everything, I walked them out to the car and made sure he was strapped in good. I gave my baby boy a kiss on the forehead. I never knew a tiny person like this could just come in and takeover putting so much love in my heart. It wasn't nothing I wouldn't do for my son. I kissed my mama on the cheek next and peeled off a couple of hundreds to give to her. "Let that girl go. She isn't no goddamn animal. You lucky I didn't see one bruise on her or else I'd be beating your ass and calling you in. You wanna make her suffer. I'm sure she's done enough of that living with the demons of knowing what she caused. I don't even need the full details of what happened or how it happened. I don't wanna keep reliving that."

"I hear you ma." I told her. "Let me know when you make it home."

So far, everything she was saying went in one ear and right out the other. She just didn't know how many hours I stayed up these past few nights staring at Kim sleeping trying hard not to strangle her ass. LeLe had better called me back and she better had done it soon. Funny how when my mama thought it was all on LeLe she was down for everything. She was down when I told her LeLe would probably show up to the house looking for me although she knew I really didn't have Trell. She was down with my entire play. When it was on LeLe, it was world war three around this bitch, but now since it's Kim's fault and she had a baby from me, it doesn't matter anymore. Made me question her fucking loyalty. She was just glad to have a grandchild since she's been asking forever. She didn't really give a damn how it happened.

She could be down with Kim if she wanted, but I could never be cool with her knowing that she caused so much of my pain and played the biggest role of taking my best friend away from me. Fuck that and fuck her too. I picked up the phone and called LeLe again. She didn't answer. I was trying to give her an opportunity to get some revenge. She better had hurried up before I did this shit on my own. I heard knocking on the wall snapping me out of my thoughts, which meant Kim was trying to get my attention. I exhaled long and hard through my flaring nostrils. When I opened the door, she jumped. "What?" I asked.

"Where is my baby? You let your mama leave with my baby?!" She asked with angry tears rolling down he face.

"He's my baby too. The fuck? I let him leave with his grandma. What the fuck you gone do about it?" I asked looking at he sideways. Wasn't like she could do shit about it.

"You can play with me about a lot of shit Majestic! But not my fucking son! He's a fresh eight weeks old! You still should've consulted with me! He's mine!" She used her free hand pointing to her chest. "Mine Majestic! I carried him! I had him! Alone! I went through that pain and pushed him out! I changed my life for that baby! How dare you!" She spat. She was so mad she was trembling and gone was that fear.

She wasn't scaring me though. "Yeah well, sue me. Had I known I had a kid on the way I would've done my part but you's a selfish ass bitch. Everything is about Kim. Always has been. That's why you in this predicament now."

She shook her head and tried to spit at me. It barely made it to the floor. "Fuck you!" She hissed. "I'm tired of being nice! I'm tired of apologizing sitting here feeling sorry for myself! Fuck you! You ain't gonna kill me! You would've done it already!"

It was sad she thought that. "Is that what you think?" I asked her pulling the gun from the small of my waist. Just as quick as she was talking. I had the tip of the gun in her mouth and damn near down her throat causing her to gag. Kim's eyes nearly popped out of her head. "I'll kill you bitch! Don't you ever think I wont."

She closed her eyes as I slowly removed the gun. She wasn't popping all that shit no more. I took her other hand and cuffed that one to the bed too now she was tied all the way up. I leaned down and spoke in her ear. "I'll be back bitch. Sit tight."

With that, I grabbed my keys and left the house to make my rounds. LeLe had twenty-four hours to call me back. I must've rode around all night long and made my way back home in the wee hours of the morning after checking on Junior. My mama was convinced she had it handled and I didn't need to worry. I sat in the driveway and rolled me a joint as I sat there smoking it. I thought about all the shit I had done. My devilish ass ways. All the pressure I had on my chest. I was no better than Kim. I never thought I was better. We came from the same struggle. She knew I knew this. I just hate she thought she had to do me this way.

I used the key to unlock the door and made my way inside the quiet house. My ears were met with the sounds of soft whimpering come from the room. I knew Kim was crying. I slowly made my way to the room and opened the door. There Kim was softly crying looking defeated again. I couldn't bare to watch this shit. I closed the door and went to lay on he couch. When I opened my eyes again. I was met with the sun shining in. To feed the bitch or to not feed the bitch was on my mind. I slowly walked to the room and Kim was already up. "Where's my son?" She asked looking like a devil with her red eyes and short hair sticking up all over her head.

I shook my head and frowned. She looked a fucking mess. Just cause she had an fucked up attitude, and I had the upper hand, I made my decision. Her ass could wait until later. It was time for me to start my day. I decided that I'd make Kim's ass suffer for a couple of more weeks.

Chapter 9

Leon Wells

"Baby, are you sure about this?" Kevin asked while standing in the mirror fixing the collar on his Polo shirt. "I just wanna make sure you're comfortable."

"I'm comfortable Kevin. If I wasn't, I wouldn't have invited you." I assured him. Deep down I was nervous as fuck. I had never had Kevin around everybody at one time. Tonight was a big night for LeLe and we were celebrating the closing on her restaurant. I couldn't believe she got that shit done in a matter of weeks but a nigga was proud of lil sis cause she deserved it. "It's gone be aiight."

In all honestly I felt like this was my official coming out party or something. I dared anybody to come with some slick shit though cause if they did I didn't mind putting them on they ass. "Okay, I just wanna make sure you good. I'm good. Trust me. This is more new for you than it is for me."

I hated when he started rambling and shit. That's the shit that made me even more nervous. After putting my shoes on, I stood up and walked over to him placing a kiss on his lips to stop him from talking. "Let it go."

Kevin immediately shut his mouth and smiled at me with his pretty ass. "I haven't spoke to LeLe in a while. She didn't even call me and let me know she had gotten the flowers for her birthday." He shrugged.

"She been hard as fuck to reach lately. Don't take it personal though. LeLe don't really fuck with her birthday like that no more."

"Why?" He frowned.

"It marks the anniversary of the day that she says fucked up her life forever."

Kevin stared at me blankly before he caught on to what I was saying. "Ohhhh. Damn, okay yeah you're right. I can imagine that had to be hard." He said grabbing his keys. "Here, you can drive my car."

We walked out of my apartment together and made our way to the restaurant. This wasn't for everybody or should I say 'the public'. Tonight was really about family getting the first look before she set an grand opening date. When we pulled up, cars already parked. "What's wrong?" I asked Kevin noticing the disturbing look on his face.

"I forgot to bring her some kind of flowers, or balloons. How rude." He tried to get back in the car. "Take me back to the flower shop."

I looked down at my watch. "No." I shook my head. "Fuck no. We already late as fuck. Nah that ain't gone work."

"Well give me the keys." He said with his hand held out. "I'll go."

I put the keys in my pocket. "Nah..." my eyes bounced around the parking lot. I knew one of these Chico's or Mexicans around here had some roses they were trying to get rid of. I spotted what I was looking for. "Aye! Papi!" I signaled him to come over.

He walked over holding his bucket of red roses. Papi had on a checkerboard shirt with a pair of jeans and a missing tooth. Looked like he had been standing out here in this hot ass sun all day grinding. "You want my friend?" He asked.

"Yeah, I want Papi." I pulled off two twenties and gave them to him just so he could have some extra. I reached in the car and grabbed an fresh bottle of water that I hadn't even opened yet.

He smiled with that missing tooth showing a big ass snag tooth gap. "Thank you my friend."

I nod my head and grabbed the roses. "You welcome my friend." I told him. He scurried off after stuffing the money probably hoping that I wasn't gone change my mind about the extra. I looked at Kevin next. "Here, my friend. Here's your roses my friend."

"Stop it." He laughed.

We made our way inside of the building and I must say, we were both shocked when we saw how LeLe had the place set up. At the top in real fancy letters above the building it read 'LeLe's' in cursive lettering. On the inside it smelled like fresh paint on the walls, which were colored in a soft nude. It definitely had a woman's touch on it. In one corner there was an area where hookahs could be smoked and the middle area was where the guest would dine in. There was also a small bar area where people could order takeout and have a drink while they waited for it to be prepared. Everything looked good. I couldn't have been prouder. "This is niceeeee."

LeLe had a DJ in the place playing music and an server here to walk around giving us drinks. Trell, Abbey, and LeLe stood in the middle talking. My mama was serving appetizers and everybody else was mingling. I saw Trey in the building too, which was odd to me but support went a long ass way. "Congrats sis." I hugged LeLe and then clapped my brother up. I hugged Abbey next. I noticed all eyes on Kevin and me.

"Nigga, it's about time ya'll got here. Nigga ain't seen yo ass since the ice age." Trell frowned.

I still felt some kind of way bout this nigga getting missing, but now wasn't the time or the place. "Nah... don't fuck with my mental Trell. I'mma definitely holla at you when this over. I didn't want Kevin to feel uncomfortable as if I didn't want people to know we were together. I knew the rest of these nosy muhfuckas had heard through the grapevine. "You okay?" I asked Kevin.

He nod his head. "Yep, I'mma go get a drink." He replied before walking off after he greeted everybody. I watched him walk away and then focused back on everybody else. Trell and Abbey looked mighty fucking comfortable to me. It didn't take a rocket scientist to figure out they were together but it wasn't my business. I was just glad they worked that shit out. A flyy ass chick LeLe had bartending walked by and Trell followed with his eyes on the sly but Abbey caught that shit. She used her pointer finger lightly mushing him in the middle of his forehead.

"You better watch what you doing with yo eyes." She warned with a chuckle but we all knew she was serious.

Trell furrowed his brows. "Told you bout puttin' yo fuckin' hands on me. I'mma snap ya lil skinny ass duck neck one day. Keep it up." He walked away.

LeLe laughed. "I don't have shit to do with that." She yelled behind the bartender. "Thanks Bari! I appreciate that."

The girl smiled and kept walking. "Who is that?" I questioned. LeLe didn't even fuck with females like that so I assumed it was some kind of company she hired.

She pointed. "Oh that's Trey's cousin Bari, she went to school with us." Then she pointed to another girl. "That's her best friend Bambi. And the one over there by the door with Trey is Trey's cousin Gu' wife Qui."

"Whew it's a whole lotta Trey's people here girl, but I ain't mad at ya." Abbey giggled.

LeLe gave Abbey a looked and pulled her to the side. I didn't know what all that was about but I took this time to finally introduce Kevin to my mama since George wasn't here. He probably wasn't feeling well again cause I know he wouldn't have missed this. I walked up behind Kevin and grabbed him by the hand leading him over to where my mama was standing. "Sup beautiful lady?" I tapped her on the shoulder so she could turn around. When she did. Her smile went to un-comfortableness upon seeing us holding hands. I guess this was something she had to get used to. It was one thing knowing about it and another to actually see it. "Hey son." She smiled and then hugged me.

She gave Kevin a quick glance up and down. "You must be Kevin?"

Kevin dropped my hand so he could shake hers. "I'm a hugger, but I don't want you to be uncomfortable." He told her. "Hi, I'm Kevin, and you're beautiful. I would've never known you had adult children." He told her.

That made her blush. I guess that's the shit that made any woman blush. "Thank you Kevin." She replied. She stared in his face for a few seconds. "My God, your eyes. I didn't expect you to be so... soo... pretty." She said.

"Thank you..." He replied. I know Kevin ain't really like being referred to as 'pretty'. He would prefer handsome but he wasn't gone address ma dukes about it. Especially when he was trying to get on her good side. Her eyes quickly scanned the room to see who was looking at us but in all honesty at this point, nobody was paying us any attention. I excused myself to go find the restroom and when I came back out I bumped into Trey and LeLe in the hall. Trey had a handful of LeLe's ass in the palm of his hands and she was on her toes giving him a peck on the lips.

"Oh my fault." I told them both. I clapped Trey up next. "What up."

"Ain't nothin'." He clapped me up nodding his head. I didn't know how I felt about this shit with Trey and LeLe. I didn't know much about dude besides he was solid but at the same time, I didn't want my sister out here looking like a hoe since she fucked with Cass first. Everybody knew them niggas used to be together.

"LeLe, let me holla at you real quick." I asked her.

She looked as if she was thinking about it.

"Go ahead." Trey told her. "I'mma be by the door ma." He walked off without a care in the world. He was like that though. He wasn't doin' too much to be liked or none of that shit. He lived in his own world.

LeLe leaned her back up against the wall. "What's wrong Leon? You okay?" She asked with concern.

I nod my head in the direction that Trey had just went. "So you and Trey huh?"

She smiled and nod her head. "Yeah." She sighed. "I'm tryna get my happy place back."

I shook my head. "I don't like it. Ion know about this shit."

She furrowed her brows looking offended and that was the last thing I was tryna do. I didn't wanna offend her. "I don't like the idea of you being gay either but I accept it. What has Trey ever done to you?"

"Nothing. That nigga ain't never done shit to nobody that I know of. Probably bodied a few niggas. That ain't the issue LeLe."

She fold her arms across her chest. "So what's the issue then Leon?"

"The issue is, I'm a nigga and ion want nobody out here in these streets tryna dog my sister's name. Everybody know you was fucking with that nigga Cass. Everybody knew Trey and Cass used to be together and now that Cass locked up you runnin' round here with Trey. I'm just saying. I'mma rock wit'chu regardless but I just don't want you to be out here lookin' crazy. If you happy, I'm happy for you."

"Leon, I'm not a murderer but everybody thinks that about me. To society I'm a felon. I can't even get a decent job; but in reality, I'm a good person. If I had to depend on what society thought in order to live. I'd never be happy again." She told me with tears in her eyes.

I pulled her in for a hug wrapping my arms around her. "Aiight sis. A nigga love you. You know that. I just wanna make sure you aiight."

"I'm okay Leon. Trust me." She smiled using the back of her hands to wipe her eyes. "Where's Kevin?"

"I left him with mama."

Her eyes got big. "You did what? Oh Lord, let me go get that man. You know how her nerves are. She's still tryna take it all in. I guarantee she has to smoke a cigarette after that."

"It is what it is." I told her watching her walk away feeling like a proud lil brother. Her eyes scanned the room for my mama but before she could take more than a few feet, Majestic walked through the door. Him and LeLe immediately locked eyes. I didn't know what that was about but when he gave her the flowers he was holding, I assumed he was here for support. As long as he didn't start no shit, I was cool with that. I felt the small of my back where my gun was tucked to feel it. I didn't trust Majestic like Trell did. I'd bust his ass in a heartbeat if he tried my sister.

Chapter 10

Leandra 'LeLe' Wells

I almost thought I saw a fucking ghost when Majestic walked in. I grabbed the flowers from him and tried to keep it cool. "If you're here, where's Kim?" I asked. I hadn't had time to think about much of her ass. I had a lot going on and a lot to lose but that didn't mean that I forgot. I hoped she was suffering good.

Majestic's eyes scanned the room before he said anything else. "This is nice. Dope as fuck actually. Congrats." He told me.

"Thanks." I mumbled. "Now where is she? Where's that baby?"

"I got it covered. I'll meet you tonight with the location. She gotta go, this is happenin' kidd."

"Do you really have it covered? Cause Karter has called me multiple times looking for her. I can't believe you haven't let her call home." I growled.

He looked at me crazy. "To say what? She's being held against her will? The fuck I look like?" He then walked around me. "Tonight LeLe. I mean that shit. With or without you."

I swallowed hard trying to ignore the thickness of the lump in my throat. Nobody had lost more than me in this entire situation, not even Majestic. Lord knows if some revenge needed to be done, it should be me doing it. I looked at everything around me at this moment and appreciated the fact that I was rebuilding. Was Kim worth me losing everything that I worked so hard and slaved for? No more rejection from jobs. No more slaving at McDonald's. No more worrying about getting fired and shit. I had become my own boss and I had to thank Trey for pushing me and not allowing me to settle cause that's where a lot of us went wrong at. We got comfortable thinking that we couldn't do any better and that wasn't always the case.

"You aiight?" Trell walked up on me causing me to jump snapping me from my thoughts.

"Yeah, I'm okay Trell." I smiled.

He reached in his pocket and passed me an envelope. "I wanted to get you something for the restaurant but you know a nigga ain't good with that kind of shit."

I opened the envelope. It was full of one hundred dollar bills. Using my fingers, I fanned through the money. "Aww thanks Trell, you know you didn't have to get me anything." I beamed.

"Nah, I wanted to. If a nigga had to be in the streets making risk, it gotta be for somebody. Why not let it be for the people you love? I'm proud of you sis." He hugged me. Trell wasn't an emotional or soft ass nigga so I really appreciated his gesture. I had a few more pieces of equipment that I needed and he had just gave me the money for it. What a blessing. I wanted to thank Trey as well cause although I used my own money, he did add a few extra things in here using his own. I was proud of myself knowing that I did something for myself that nobody could take away from me. When it was time for a toast, I had my water in my hand because I still wasn't ready to drink yet. I couldn't take the anxiety. After the toast, it was over and eventually the crowd thinned out leaving Trey and me alone. I locked up and turned around to find Trey. He was sitting at the bar with a shot of Hennessy in his glass cup. This was the first time I'd ever seen him drink. I took my heels off and slide my feet into some Gucci slides before ignoring a call from Majestic.

Trey was intensely staring at me. I had those butterflies again, but at the same time, I wanted to hop on his dick. I hadn't had sex in three years and that felt like a lifetime. I was almost positive that I was a born again virgin. "What's wrong?' I smiled at him wrapping both my arms around his neck.

He took a swig and put the glass back down. "I'm proud of you ma. Foreal."

"I have you to thank baby."

He shook his head and pulled me closer to him. "Nah, you did this. A man can lead and it's up to that woman to follow. You did that and look where it got you. I ain't gone never steer you wrong."

I closed my eyes and slowly exhaled. *Lord, I hope this is the one for me.* I thought to myself. When I opened my eyes, Trey spoke to me again. "What kinda waitin' to exhale type of shit you on ma? Don't tell me you prepared to start lightin' fires round this bitch too." He joked. I couldn't believe how he was slowly opening up to me. I doubt many people saw this side of Trey. I felt so lucky.

I tilt my head to the side ready to ask him some questions, but then I pierced my lips together to stop from asking knowing how much he hated questions. I guess he peeped.

"Spit it out shorty." He told me. The way he grabbed me. The strength in his grip. The certainty in his words. The confidence in his hustle, it all intrigued me and had me wanting him even more.

"You still trying to move to Atlanta Trey? I need to know. Seriously."

"Why?"

"Cause that's gonna play a big factor in our relationship Trey. I need to know. I don't want you to hype me up just to turn around and leave me. I can't take another heartbreak and I can't be played with Trey."

He gave me a deep glare with those dark brown eyes. "Do it look like I'm playin' wit' you baby girl? You think a nigga went through all of this to play wit'chu? It's plenty bitches out here I can play wit' ma. Why choose you?"

I guess that was definitely something to think about. He was right. Why choose me? "Speaking of, why did you choose me Trey?"

"The question is, why not choose you? You don't think you worth that?" He asked looking at me sideways. I could smell the Hennessy coming off of his warm breath. As usual, his cologne tickling my nose. I didn't answer him. He continued. "Look I'm willin' to be everything you need me to be, but if you fuck over me. I'mma kill you. I'mma bury yo ass right in the middle of the rock pit." He said holding his chest. "On everything ma. My loyalty runs deep. I don't play those kinda games. This why I don't let people get close to me."

I laughed, but Trey had a hidden type of crazy about him. He was one of those niggas that would get the job done and move on like it never happened. I felt this. This is why he was so reserved and always observing people. "I think you know I'm not like that, or I wouldn't be here right now. I still need you to answer my question. Are you leaving me?"

"Nah baby girl. You my only reason to stay. That and I can't leave my nephew."

"What's going on with that anyway? Where is he?"

"Not in the system no more. My parents got him. I just provide financially. I don't fuck with them like that."

"Why not?"

"Long story ma. Just know, they favored CoCo over me and she end up being the fucked up one. It is what it is."

"Will I meet them?"

"Doubt it." He shrugged.

My phone was vibrating again in my hand. I frowned and silenced it. Sucking my teeth, I wished Majestic would've just let me have this night.

"Everything aiight?" Trey asked me. I guess suspecting that something was wrong.

"I'm fine." I mumbled.

I knew he saw that was Majestic calling and from my observations, previously, I don't think he fucked with him like that either. He never treated him like a friend. I'm sure he didn't trust him either. "You ready?" He asked me.

"Yeah, let me just grab my purse." I told him rushing behind the bar to grab my purse. Trey grabbed me by the hand and walked me out. "So where we going now?" I asked looking at my watch. "It's still early. We gotta celebrate."

"Come on." He led me to his truck stopping at the passenger door to open it for me. When he got in the driver seat, he gave me a jewelry box. "This for you ma. You doin' big things now. You on yo Boss shit so it's only right."

I smiled with anticipation wondering what it was. Much to my surprise, it was the twin version of his Cartier watch, just made for a female. "Oooouuu you did ya big one. I love it Trey." I beamed. I put it back in the box and rest my head back on the seat to relax after adjusting the air vents directly in my face.

I didn't know where we were headed to, but I was on a cloud. I grabbed my phone from my purse and powered it off cause I didn't wanna be bothered. As far as I was concerned, fuck Majestic right now and fuck Kim's rat ass too. It wasn't until we pulled up to a big family home that I realized I was in Miami Lakes. "Who lives here?" I asked.

He walked around and let me out the truck. "Just come on." He held my hand leading me to the front door. It wasn't until he pulled out the house key and let us in did I realize that it was his house. It was beautiful and low key as hell. I would've never found this house since it's on a back road in a small sub-division. "It's my house."

"Whattt?" I clapped playfully. "I finally made it to your house? Oh hell yeah. I'm definitely in there." I gave him a playful fist pound.

He shook his head and chuckled. "Yo ass crazy." Flicking on the lights, he walked to the kitchen and placed his keys on the island.

"Wait a minute." I frowned. "You don't have no furniture in here. How long you been living here?"

He shrugged. "For awhile now. I was hardly ever here before when I was movin' the bread, but I'm chillin' now. It's time to make this house a home."

"Why didn't you at least start little by little?"

He popped the top off of the Corona bottle that he grabbed out the fridge. "Maybe I was waitin' on you baby girl. A nigga don't decorate and allat. That aint really my thing. All I needed was some bedroom furniture and I'm good."

I walked to the fridge. "You don't even have no groceries. You don't cook?" I asked.

"When I wanna cook, I go buy it." He let me know.

I slammed the fridge door back closed. "Nah, that's unacceptable." I told him. "When the last time you had a woman cook for you?"

Trey sat at the one barstool at the island. "I don't have company and ion trust females. The last chick that cooked for me was my first girlfriend and she couldn't cook for shit. After that, I said fuck it and taught myself. Nigga got tired of feeding her food to my pit-bull back then."

I bust out laughing. "You so wrong for that."

This was the first time I had ever heard him mention anything about a girlfriend and it made me feel a certain kinda way although it was way before me. "So what happened?"

"With what?"

"The ex-girlfriend? Why didn't it work out?" I asked.

"Come on ma. Don't tell me you about to start with the 21 questions."

"Closed mouths don't get fed Trey. How am I supposed to know if you don't tell me?"

He stood up and checked his phone. "I mean, it ain't nothin' I really wanna talk about. The shit ain't work. She wanted more and I couldn't give it to her so that was that. We still cool though."

"Ohh I see." I said.

He stroked his goatee and took another swig from his bottle. "So wussup wit' you and that nigga Majestic?" He asked catching me off guard. "I peep the exchange between ya'll earlier. I read yo body language ma. That tells it all."

I scrunched my face up. "You think I'm fucking with Majestic?"

"I would hope not, that some real crazy ass shit there, but I know you ain't like that. I'm askin' cause I know all about that nigga puttin' Poochie on you in hopes of him fuckin' yo life up. Ion trust that nigga. If he fuckin' wit'chu, that's somethin' I need to know."

I thought back to everything that happened with Cass. I wish it would've never happened. I can't say I regretted meeting him. In fact, because of him giving me that job, I was able to get a jumpstart on stacking my bread and opening my business. If it wasn't for Cass, I wouldn't have met Trey, the nigga I was supposed to be with. If it were anything I regretted, it was being so damn gullible, but being fresh out of prison, I was desperate to come up and I may have indeed been a little too trusting even when I knew better. I couldn't tell Trey about the whole Kim situation, this was Majestic and I's problem. "No, it's nothing like that. We're just trying to move forward. We've both been through a lot."

"Aiight, I'mma leave it at that." He told me walking away. I followed him through the big empty house as the sounds of our shoes echoed through the house. He had one simple sectional in the living room and that's it. He opened the double door that led to his bedroom. As soon as he opened it up, it looked like a house all in itself. It was nothing like the rest of the house. His room was fit for a king. The huge King Poster bed was decorated with gold and black sheets as well as the rest of the décor in his room. He had a huge walk-in closet and the bathroom was big enough to fit an small gathering of people. I was in complete awe. Hell, I took off my slides at the door and sat them outside of the door allowing my feet to sink down into his plush carpet. It was much more welcoming than the rest of the house, which was filled with tile and marble.

"I like this. It's so bomb." I complimented him. Everything was in order and nothing looked out of place. It was so clean. "I can't wait until it's time for me to get a house. I'm just tryna help my parent's as much as possible right now. Can I sit?" I asked not just wanting to sit on his bed without asking. It was made up so nicely I didn't wanna fuck it up.

"Come on baby girl. I look like a boujee ass nigga? Yeah you can sit down." He told me kicking his shoes off and placing them in the closet. Her removed his jeans next, and then his shirt leaving only his Polo boxers and his wife beater tee on his body along with his socks. My eyes scanned his chocolate body from top to bottom. His calf muscles were so masculine and perfectly defined. His biceps, his 6-pack, everything about this man was beautiful. I licked my lips not even being shy about it. "Don't be tryna start some shit you ain't gone finish or cant handle." He flopped on the bed next to me and grabbed the remote.

"Whatever." I chuckled. "Soooo, it's getting late and I'd like to get comfortable too but unfortunately you didn't tell me we were coming here and I didn't bring a change of comfortable clothes with me. I don't wanna be stuck in this skirt and blouse."

Trey stopped flipping the channels and looked at me. "Take it off then."

"Say what?" I asked with a raised brow.

"We ain't kids ma. If it's uncomfortable take it off. You can wear ya panties and bra. I'm not gone do shit to you that you don't want done, trust me. I know ion look like the type of nigga to steal some pussy. Had you had to work tomorrow, I would've taken you home, but you yo own boss now shorty, and you make yo own rules."

I don't know why I felt like a little shy ass girl instead of a grown ass woman. Besides, I didn't have shit to be ashamed about. My body was stacked. He knew it and so did everybody else around me. Slowly standing up, I unzipped my skirt and pulled my shirt off making sure to fold it and sit it on the dresser. I did the same for my blouse. The cold air from the AC unit caused my body to softly shiver now that I was exposed wearing nothing besides my black mesh thong with the matching bra. I hurriedly slid under the covers as Trey watched me. Ass jiggling and all. Trey got up and slid up under the heavy comforter with me wrapping his strong arms around me allowing me to lay on his chest.

All of a sudden, I felt nervous as hell. I needed to find something to talk about. I needed to do it quickly too. "Trey, I've been thinking about my new recipe, or should I say my new recipes. I have so much stuff that I wanna try and…"

"LeLe…" He said in the most serious tone I'd heard him use tonight.

I stopped talking since he cut me off anyway. "Oh, I'm sorry. I'm rambling huh?"

"I don't wanna talk about no recipes tonight ma."

I pulled my face up from his chest and looked him in the face. He wasn't playing. He wasn't looking mean either. He looked at me with so much lust in his eyes. He didn't have to say shit to me cause his facial expression said it all. Slowly, I placed my lips against his and slowly kissed him allowing my tongue to disappear in his mouth. I mounted my body on top of his straddling him before leaning down into the kiss again. Trey had his hands placed on my plump ass and I felt his hard dick growing up under me causing my panties to instantly cream. I knew it, I felt it. This was the touch that I missed so much. This was nothing like prison making fake dildos to please ourselves with. This was the real deal here and I knew I wasn't making a mistake by giving myself to Trey. He allowed me to take lead at first but after I slowly licked on his neck, he pulled each of my breast from my bra and gently sucked on my brown Hershey kiss like nipples where he flickered his tongue over them before popping it into his mouth. "Ouuuu." I moaned slowly grinding my hips over his hard dick causing me to immediately rupture and have a light orgasm. My entire body felt hot at this point. Trey flipped me over on my back and spread my legs wide over his shoulder. He didn't say anything as I panted in anticipation of feeling his tongue on my awaiting pussy.

Trey didn't even try to attempt to get my thong off, instead, he ripped the thin fabric from my body before exposing my freshly waxed pussy. Using his tongue, he gently brushed it across my swollen nub where he focused for the first few seconds gently sucking on it causing me to buck my hips into his rhythm. I was so fucking wet, I could feel the puddle up under me fucking his sheets up but neither one of us cared as he studied my body bringing my feet up to his broad shoulders and digging back in. "Shhhh." I whined. "Ouuu Trey, right there. Right there." I moaned rolling my eyes in the back of my head.

They way he took his hands and placed them on my hips to keep me in place had me about to go crazy as he focused on that spot right above the clitoris. The spot that I was sure only us women knew about. He definitely knew something. Trey brought me to another orgasm as I bucked my hips allowing my walls to contract. The sounds of him lightly slurping my juices turned me the fuck on. When he made sure he had satisfied me there. He came up and pulled his boxers off along with his white tee exposing his ripped chest and his huge monster dick. I mean, the shit literally hung like a horse and I tensed up just looking at it. "You wanna stop?" He asked me noticing how I tensed up.

I shook my head still panting. "No." I told him reaching up bringing him back down to me before placing a kiss on his mouth tasting my own juices. Trey spread my legs as far as I would allow him to go before reaching over to his nightstand drawer pulling out a condom and sliding it on his dick. I thought Malik had a big dick but he didn't have shit on Trey. This was wild as hell. I'm surprised he didn't have bitches knocking his door down. I'm surprised his ex let him go with a dick like this. It was hard to find a good-sized dick out here and this was definitely one.

Trey gently eased his way into my awaiting honey pot slowly because he knew my situation and he knew I hadn't had sex in years. I thanked God I was fully lubricated and wet down there with my own juices cause that was a big help and contribution to him not hurting me. The further he went, the more it hurt. I felt like I was getting my cherry popped all over again as the tears burned my eyes. I bit down on my bottom lip. "You want me to stop?" Trey whispered in my ear before nuzzling his nose in my neck licking that weak spot.

"No." I panted.

He went further until he was filling me up and when he was finally in, it wasn't so bad anymore but I swore I saw the stars, the moon, the sun, outer space and all that good shit as we learned each others body. Trey used the hook of his dick to stroke me long and hard and then hard and slow working my ass like no other had before. Every time he would pull out I would feel a gush of my juices. If I had to describe it, it would be like the sounds of somebody mixing up a bowl of mac and cheese. I tried to ease back a little but Trey pulled me back to him placing both my legs over his shoulders. "Oh my Goddddd." I groaned watching his stomach muscles flex as he stared down at my bare pussy watching his dick move in and out of it. He used his free hand to place two fingers on my swollen nub while he played with it bringing me right back to a long and hard orgasm. I could tell Trey was trying to contain himself and that thick vein that popped out in the middle of his forehead was sexy as fuck as he concentrated on pleasing me. "Treyyyy." I whined. "I cant cum again. Oh myyyy. Ouuuuu."

"Yes you can ma." He groaned looking at me with those deep browns. "You gone cum for me again ma?" He asked not giving me a chance to respond before he was flipping me over placing his hand on the small of my back so he can get me in a position to give him a deep arch while I was on all fours doggy style. When he slid into me, I almost fucking fainted. At first, it was painful because his dick had to stretch me out in this position but after a few strokes I was throwing the pussy back at him looking like a bobble head. I had my hair blown out by the Dominican's earlier but I just knew my shit was frizzed up and threw now since I didn't get perms. The sweat trickled down from my forehead.

Smack!

Trey smacked my ass causing a light sting. In a good way. In fact, he made my pussy wetter. "You gone cum for me ma?" He asked again as he lightly groaned. "Come on…"

I didn't know if it was because I felt his dick get even harder and stiffen up, which let me know that he was about to cum too, or if it was the smacking of my ass, or just if it was simply because he was working the shit out of my pussy but just like he demanded, I was cumming for him again. "Ahhhhh!" I closed my eyes and yelled out in pleasure. "Malikkkk I'm cummingggg." I whined.

"Me too ma…" he pumped faster before gripping my hips holding me in place allowing his semen to rupture through the condom. "Fuckkkk!" He let it out and stayed just like that for a few seconds. Trey leaned down and kissed the nape of my neck before rolling over on his back. I wanted to place my head on his chest, but he didn't allow me and I knew why. I had just fucked up big time. I didn't know what to say. Neither one of us had any words. I watched Trey get up and go to the bathroom as I clung the sheets up against my body.

When he came back out, he didn't even look at me. He slipped his shit back on. "Trey…" I called his name in a low voice. I was so embarrassed. "Trey, I'm sorry. I didn't mean to…" I stopped talking and sighed before I finished. "I didn't mean that."

"Look ma. Had you been any other female I'd be kickin' you out my shit right now but due to yo delicate situation I'm tryin' my best to let that ride. I'm not gone compete with a dead man. Ain't no way I can do that. You gotta figure it out." He told me leaving me in the room alone. I could've crawled up under a rock and died. That's how embarrassed I was. I don't even know why I said that. I wasn't even thinking about Malik in that moment. Trey had given me everything a woman can ask for in the bed so far and I insulted him. I felt like shit.

I was hoping that Trey would come back in the room, but after an hour, I figured he wasn't coming back so I crept into the bathroom and cleaned myself off before putting my clothes back on. I went to go find Trey, he was on the couch sleeping on his back with his gun on his lap. I slowly crept back into the room and powered my phone on. I needed to leave. I couldn't be up when he got up and faced him after saying that stupid shit. I had a text from Majestic and I needed to call him back realizing that he wasn't gonna let this go, and I couldn't keep running.

I called him back and let him know I was on my way to the warehouse. I called an Uber next. When they arrived, I made sure I locked the bottom lock and hopped in taking the ride to the warehouse. Majestic was on my last fucking nerve. He went from hating me to acting like he owned me. He knew he didn't give a shit whether or not I had anything to do with this. He just wanted to feel like he had some kind of control, he just wanted to be an asshole. I couldn't stand it. I hopped out of the car and went inside the warehouse. The temperature had dropped drastically but it had been doing that lately in the wee hours of the morning for the past few nights.

I knocked and he hit the buzzard to let me in. "I'm here." I frowned when I saw him. I frowned even harder when I saw Kim, she looked like shit and I didn't feel sorry for her ass. It looked like Majestic had been taking her through it. She had lost a few pounds. Her previously glowing skin just looked pale and her hair was all over the place.

"It's about fucking time." He scolded me. "I got the van in the back. Let's go." He said giving me a pair of gloves to put on. Now I was feeling nervous taking the damn gloves from him. This wasn't what my life was about. Since he had tape around Kim's mouth, she couldn't even say shit but the tears that rolled down her face said all of her words. She didn't wanna die and I knew she was only allowing him to do the things that he had done to her was because of her baby. She didn't even try to beg or scream, she just looked sympathetic with her eyes.

I let Majestic take Kim out to the van he had and then I followed behind him and hopped in the passenger seat behind the tints. Kim couldn't move in the back of the van because he made sure he had her cuffed. "Where we going?" I asked irritated ready to get this shit over with. Whatever he was gonna do if he wanted to witness it then what the fuck ever. It just needed to get done.

"Somewhere where nobody will ever find this bitch." He replied. My heart dropped after that. I kept asking myself what the fuck I was doing in this van. Did I hate Kim that fucking much? The answers was, yes I did, but I wasn't a killer and I didn't want to ever have shit come back on me that would even have me locked up. I felt sick in the pit of my stomach thinking that I was already in too deep at the point of no return. Majestic was doing exactly what he wanted to do and that was have me uncomfortable to feel like he had something over my head. We rode in silence cause I didn't have shit to say to him. He drove us out west to an outdoor gun field where people normally came for target practice. Wasn't shit out here besides trees and shit. Kinda reminded me of the wilderness.

When we found the spot he was looking for, he put the van in park and then went to the back to let Kim out. She didn't even have on any shoes as she landed on her feet in the dirt and grass when she got out. Gone were the tears, she finally was ready to accept her fate. When we locked eyes, the only thing I could make out in them was another apology since she couldn't physically say it. Majestic looked like he was all too excited about this for my liking. He led Kim deeper into the trees holding her by one arm real aggressive, which he didn't have to cause at this point, she wasn't even putting up an fight. I didn't know how far we had to walk, but Majestic finally stopped in front of a hole in the dirt that he had apparently already dug out. Using force, he slung Kim to the ground and pointed the gun toward her head. My heart was pounding so fucking fast. This shit wasn't right. No matter what happened, it just wasn't.

I wasn't this cold ass person like Majestic was and I refused to let him turn me into that. Kim was on her knees with her eyes closed and her back turned away from us trembling awaiting her fate. Majestic cocked the gun and looked at me for approval. "Wait!" I stopped him with tears in my eyes.

He frowned. "What? Now aint the time for this shit LeLe." He growled looking like a deranged man. I saw through that shit. Deep down inside, he loved Kim. However, he felt like he would be betraying Malik to let her live.

I sighed. "I'll do it." I reached for his gun. "Give it to me. I'll do it. You go watch our fucking backs. If something happens or if somebody rolled up on us it isn't shit I can do to protect or save us. You can." I explained. "Give it to me."

"Fuck no!" He disagreed.

"Majestic, nobody has loss more than me in this entire situation. You owe this to me. I owe this to Malik. Let me do it." I told him again a little softer this time. It took him a few seconds to think about it but he eventually passed me the 9mm gun. It was awfully heavy, but I knew I could handle it. "Just go, I got it."

"Make it quick." He told me before walking over to Kim. She jumped when he spoke into her ear. "See you on the dark side bitch."

He then walked away. With a single tear in my eye. I walked up to the back of Kim's head.

Pow!

One single bullet was all I had to fire. One single bullet still couldn't erase a lifetime of pain.

"How you feelin'?" Majestic asked me when I got back in the van. I didn't even realize that my hands were shaking uncontrollably. I didn't realize that the fresh tears were still on my face.

"Fine." I mumbled. I didn't wanna talk to his sick ass. I didn't see how this was even enjoyable to him. Just get me back the warehouse. I'll Uber home."

"I can take you. It ain't that deep."

"No!" I snapped. "I don't need the ride."

He didn't say shit else besides when it was time for me to get out of the van. He grabbed my arm prompting me to look at him like I smelled some shit on the bottom of a shoe. I snatched my arm away. "What?"

"Don't tell nobody about this shit or I'll have to come back and kill yo ass." He warned before allowing me to get out.

"Yeah, yeah aiight. I got it. I know the rules." I replied sarcastically before getting out and hopping in my Uber since they arrived the same time. I needed to fucking think. When I got in the Uber, I had the driver to take me home. I was so shaken up that I didn't know what to do as I tried to get my emotions together. It was well after 4 in the morning and I didn't want to wake anybody up. Trell wasn't even here so I assumed he was with Abbey. I decided to take me a quick shower riding myself of any stench of sex and then sent Trey a text message before that he would see when he woke up. *Trey, I first want to say thank you for everything. In a short period of time, you have managed to bring so much joy and pureness to my heart. I respect you so much as a man because you have done so much to prove you are just that. I made a huge mistake tonight and I can't apologize enough but I promise if you let me, I wanna make it up to you. My intentions are never to make you compete with my past. I'm just work in progress with letting the past go. I locked the door behind me when I left because I couldn't bare to face you when you awoke. I hope you understand. I'll call you in a few hours. Goodnight/morning Trey.*

I tried so hard to fall asleep after that but my stomach was in knots as if I wanted to vomit just replaying everything from tonight. Visions of Kim clouded my mind. I thought I'd feel better after making her suffer, truth was. It was the complete opposite.

Chapter 11

Leandra 'LeLe' Wells

Trey never text me back so I went ahead to the restaurant and decided to just do some cleaning and come up with some recipes when I woke up. I had so much on my list that I wanted to do and I needed to keep my mind busy so I called Abbey to see if she could come up since I knew she wasn't working. "I'm coming girl." She yawned. "You gotta give me like an hour though cause a bitch is tired. All Trell and me do is fuck like rabbits."

I frowned and removed the phone away from my ear before placing it back. "What the fuck? Bitch I don't wanna hear no shit like that ever again referring to my brother. That's just too fucking much. You done messed everything up. We cant even gossip about niggas and stuff cause the one you wanna talk about is related to me."

"Yeah, I guess that is kinda awkward huh?' She chuckled. "Aiight I'm coming though, I'll be there. I need a few cooking lessons anyway."

"Good. I need you to be a taster for me and I gotta tell you something."

"What?" She asked all turned up a notch. "You gave Trey some of that cobweb pussy didn't you?"

"Ummhmmm." I replied in a teasing way.

"Omgggg!" She laughed. "And I wanna know all the details blow by blow."

"Now come on Abbey, you know good girls never tell."

"Good girl my ass." She responded trying to rush off the phone. "Make me a breakfast sandwich or something. Pleaseeee LeLe?"

I just giggled and shook my head. "I got you."

When she arrived, I had the sandwich waiting for her as promised and I let her in and then locked the door so people wouldn't think I was open and serving. Abbey's skin was glowing and she looked well refreshed walking in looking all pretty with a yellow and blue sundress clinging perfectly to her light skin. Her hair short hair was wrapped in the matching scarf and she wore huge gold-hooped earrings in her ears. Her freckles were popping and so was the nude lipstick she wore.

Abbey gave me a hug and I sat the sandwich down in front of her. "Hey girl." She bit into it and then closed her eyes allowing them to roll in the back of her head being dramatic. "This is so fucking good." She complimented my homemade breakfast sandwich on a buttery croissant. In between the sandwich was maple bacon, fried smoked sausage, a fried egg, grilled onions, and pepper jack cheeses. I That was one that I thought about adding on the menu as well.

"I'm glad you like it." I told her wiping down the counter. I had a jukebox in the corner that I went and played some music on. My legs were so sore that it hurt to even walk back and forth from there.

"Damn, Trey got you walking like that?" She asked still munching on her food not missing a beat. "Must've been a monster dick girl."

"You have no idea girl. I'm gonna soak in some Epsom salt today. I cant take it." I sighed. "That's not what all I wanted to tell you though."

She raised a brow and wiped her mouth with a single napkin. "What did you do?"

It was no easy way to say it, so I told her. "I fucked up and called him Malik."

"And you still have all your teeth? Bitchhhhh. That's wild."

"Why you always have to just add salt on an open wound Abbey?" I asked. "Of course I still have all my teeth but he made it very clear if I had been any other female that he would've been putting me the fuck out. I couldn't face him after that so I left on my own."

"That was dumb." She let me know as she took another bite.

"What?"

"Leaving. That was dumb as hell. You should've stayed. Would've showed him that you were genuine ya know? That you ain't the type to run when it gets hard. That was probably a test and your ass failed badly."

I didn't think about the way she was putting it until now. When I left, I left cause I had some personal shit to handle, but at the same time, had I stayed, I wouldn't have ended up where I did last night doing something I really didn't wanna do. I thought about telling Abbey what happened with Kim but I didn't wanna keep talking about it. It was time to move on and heal. "I didn't think about it like that. What do you think I should do?" I asked her.

She shrugged. "Do how you do everybody else. Cook for him." She suggested. I thought about it briefly and I decided I would do just that. When I left here, I would go ahead and pick up some groceries for his place and cook him a good ass meal. I hoped he allowed me and didn't reject me. I thought calling Abbey here would help ease my mind, but no matter what I did, my mind kept going back to Kim. Maybe she didn't deserve what she had endured. I felt for that baby as well, but I knew I could never have any dealings with him. The entire situation was just too damn tough for me. "Something else is on your mind though. What's wrong?"

I wanted to tell Abbey, but I knew I couldn't, at least not now. "Nothing." I shrugged. "Just tired, I guess."

"What's the deal with Kim?" She asked.

"Why we talking about Kim?"

"Cause I'm worried about her. In all honesty, I don't want shit to happen to her and you know Majestic's ass ain't all the way there. No telling what he's doing to that girl."

It was burning me up how she just completely forgot what Kim had done to me. I wouldn't bring it up though. I would push it as far back in my mind as possible. "Look, I have to go okay. I'll call you later."

"Are you putting me out?" She asked shocked.

"I'm not being rude." I said looking at my watch. "I really gotta go." I checked my phone and had already had three missed calls from my mama and needed to call her back. I knew she probably wanted to know how the rest of my night went before I got home. Abbey and me hugged it up one more time before I locked up and rushed out to my car. On the way to the house, I called her back but she didn't answer. When I finally pulled up to the house, it ambulance was here shocking the shit out of me. Trell and Leon were here too. I turned my car off and rushed through the front door. George immediately fell on my mind. "Maaa!" I opened the door and rushed to the back room. From what I could see, they were working on George. He laid lifeless on the bed and his shirt was ripped open. Trell was consoling my mama and Leon stood off to the side looking like he was in shock.

"What's going on?!" I asked with tears in my eyes trying to rush to George's side. "Georgeeee!" I cried. He wasn't responding to me.

"He's gone! I know he's gone!" My mama wailed into Trell's chest. Trell just looked at me helpless with pain in his eyes. Leon grabbed me holding me into a bear hug.

"He's gone sis..." He softly cried. "He's gone..."

"What the fuck? Noooooo!" I screamed a blood hurdling scream from the depths of my soul. George couldn't be dead. No way. I knew he hadn't been feeling well but he always pulled through. Always. I couldn't decipher what happened next because I blacked the fuck out. Like I could see what was going on, but everything was a blur to me. It literally was moving in slow motion as

I sat on the couch in Leon's arms. I wanted to talk, but nothing would come out. I wanted to hold George when they removed his lifeless body from the house. I wanted to tell my mama it would be okay, although I knew it wouldn't. This would never be okay.

This brought me back to the passing of Malik. This was a pain that I didn't think I would feel again so soon. I hated it so much. I was sure when it was my time to go, it would be from a broken heart because God had truly taken two huge chunks of my heart away from me. I thought George would be fine after his surgery, I thought he would pull through. Apparently, the same surgery that saved his life also caused him to die from complications. I couldn't take this shit at all. It was just too much. How was I supposed to plan a funeral? I couldn't, I was just too weak to do that. My mama was devastated, but she was a strong woman. She refused to stay home with us. She made sure she went with George's body to make sure she could have everything set. Trell went with her. The entire time she kept mumbling about how cold he was. "He so cold. He needs a blanket. Don't ya'll take him out of here without a fucking blanket." She told the coroner as they zipped him in the body bag.

I was too outdone to even get the full story but from what I gathered, Trell and my mama came home from the store and found him in the bed dead. That had to be one of the hardest things to do, to find someone that way and can't even help, especially your husband. Leon didn't say a word. He allowed me to sit with him as much as I needed to. For a minute, I almost said 'fuck God' because if he loved me so much why did he make all of these things happen to me? I had lost way too much and every time I think that it's finally going good or this is it, something happens.

For the rest of the day everything was in a blur. I didn't give a shit about who was calling my phone or texting. I was numb, like a fucking zombie. I thought about all of my childhood memories with George and how he kept this family together. A true stand up guy. Every time I walk past their room. I got sick. As the day went on, everyone piled up little by little once word got out to come and pay their respects to our family. I didn't want to be bothered with none of these fucking people though, family or not. It baffled me how by the end of the night they would all just end up drunk and it would turn into a little party. They called it celebration of life. My mama was hurting, Trell was hurting, Leon was hurting, and I was crushed. Kevin came and sat next to me on the porch and placed my hand into his. "You need anything lil sis?" He asked me. His eyes were red like he'd been crying. Kevin was hurt for our family.

With a half smile, I told him. "No."

He nod his head and still sat with me as we watched the cars ride by. Everyone else was on the inside of the house. Abbey was also in there trying her best to assist everyone and take the pressure off of my mama. Abbey was devastated about George. He did right by us all. I never known him to have not one enemy. The crew from his old job showed up as well with their condolences and although we didn't need money to pay for his funeral, they offered big donations, which was thoughtful. I wanted to call Trey, but I knew he was pissed with me. I wasn't even sure if he wanted to talk to me at this point and in all honesty, I had way too much going on.

The next week went by slow, too damn slow for my liking. I had to push back the grand opening day for the restaurant and I had to take complete control over the funeral arrangements. We didn't want our mama paying for anything so Trell, Leon, and I made sure we went all out for George and put him away nice. He didn't have any family besides us and our side of the family so that's who showed up the day of the funeral. If I had to count how many times I'd spoken to Trey up until this point, I would say a few times, but it was real brief and I didn't even mention George. I didn't want a pity party. I was tired of those. I needed to be strong for my family.

My mama had been like a zombie and I was afraid to leave her side most of the time. Trell did the best he could but he spent most of his days in the gym blowing off steam in frustration of finding of job. He had been waiting for The University of Miami Hospital to call him back in regards to a physical therapy in sports position and he was also waiting to hear back about a head coaching position at St. Thomas High School.

George's favorite thing to wear was white tee shirts and blue jeans so that's what we all decided to wear. We didn't do the whole dress up thing cause that wasn't his style. My family and I sat in front of the casket on the first row of the church while the Pastor preached through the service. The more he spoke, the more my heart crumbled in a million pieces. When it was my time to speak, I had the support of both my brothers and Abbey right by my side to console me as I got it out. Staring at the now closed casket, I couldn't believe I was saying my final goodbye to my hero. The man who raised me when the man who made me wasn't even man enough to do it. "I promised I wasn't gone get up here and cry ya'll." I sniffed.

"Take your time baby. Take your time." I heard multiple people telling me.

Abbey passed me a napkin. I used it to dab the corner of my eyes before starting again. "I have a poem I wanna read." I told them trying to hold back the tears. I started. *"George, you were truly one in a million. When God was making Fathers, as far I can see, he spent a lot of time on me, and saved that 'one' for me. He made a perfect gentleman, compassionate and kind, with more patience and affection, than you could hope to find. He gave this special person, a heart of solid gold, and after God had finished, he must've broken the mold."* I dabbed my eyes again. *"George, you were just too perfect for earth so God called you back home. Rest in heavenly peace. We Love You."* I finished and stepped down leaving everyone in tears.

When it was time to view the body one last time, I couldn't even do it. Trell and Leon stood with my mama and Abbey stood next to Trell. Kevin then went to join them as I rocked back and forth singing along with 'Take Me To The King'. I wasn't even paying attention to who came and sat next to me until I felt the strong hand inside of mine. I looked to the right of me and Trey gave me a knowing look. "I got'chu baby girl. I got'chu." He pulled me into his arms letting me break down. I was so happy to see him. I wasn't even sure how he knew about this but I was glad he showed up. I needed his comfort more than ever. This was the hardest thing I had to do outside of burying Malik. If they told me that I had to do another five years in prison just to get George back, I would do it in a heartbeat. My mama wasn't the glue that kept us together, she never was. Bingo consumed her entire life and George held us down. Even when we gave him a hard time.

"Thank you so much." I whispered to Trey when the service was over. "I'm glad you came."

"I wouldn't have had it no other way shorty." He told me kissing me on the cheek. Trell and Leon both walked up to him and clapped him up showing gratitude for him coming to pay his respects.

The repast was at a hall that Kevin had managed to rent out. It was packed as hell too, there was faces I had never even seen before. Trey immediately went into action bringing in all of the heavy shit and assisting my mama with any this that she needed although she hadn't even met him and didn't know who he was. She was just in a daze. I wasn't sure she could function with George being gone. One thing we all promised though, was that we were going to hold her down no matter what.

There was a huge projector that showed all of our pictures with George from babies up until this point. There were multiple pictures of him that we hadn't seen before either that was quite funny. George had always been a fine man with those deep hazel eyes. "You aiight?" Trey hovered over me checking on me, which he had done multiple times within' the past hour. I nod my head. "I'm okay."

He walked away again to go help do some more shit. Abbey came and sat next to me next with a plate of food in her hand. It smelled good, but nothing would allow me to eat right now. I had been picking over my food for the past few days. Even when I tried to eat it didn't work. "Bitchhhh, look who's here." She nudged me swallowing a mouthful of collard greens. My eyes focused on the front entrance where Karter was walking in with a tall white woman that I assumed to be Emily, she was beautiful too. They headed straight for us.

"Hey Queen." Karter leaned down to hug me. "How you holding up?" She asked giving me a card.

"Hi... I'm um, I'm making it. When did you get here?" I asked nervously.

She smiled. "We just got in town. There was no way we couldn't show up here. George was very nice to us all growing up." She removed her shades. "This is my fiancé Emily." She said. "Emily this is LeLe and of course you remember Abbey."

Emily extended her hand to shake mine and I did the same. "Nice to meet you. I hate it had to be under these circumstances. I'm sorry for your loss." She told me.

"Thank you for coming. I appreciate you." I told her.

She went to hug Abbey but Abbey stopped her holding her fist out to give Emily a pound. "Un Un don't even try it with that reserved shit Emily. You forgot, I know you already. You're a whole black girl under that skin." She giggled.

Emily lightly chuckled and gave Abbey a pound instead of a hug. Her eyes scanned the room. "No Kim?" She asked.

Abbey suddenly stood up and excused herself. "Look at the time." She frowned looking at her watch. "I need to start putting up pans." She rushed off.

I frowned in her direction, she knew what the fuck she was doing. How dare she leave me with them to answer questions. I guess since I wouldn't talk to her about shit, she wouldn't talk to them about shit. "No, no Kim." I said dryly and feeling bad as hell. "You know how Kim is."

I looked across the room and spotted Trey leaned up against the wall with a Corona in his hand engulfed in a conversation with my brothers. He looked at me and gave me the wink of an eye. Next, Majestic walked through the door once again holding some flowers. I wished he would've just stayed the fuck away. Majestic was too many bad memories for me, everything that I wanted to forget, he was a constant reminder. "Excuse me for a second ya'll. Kim's baby daddy just walked in." I marched toward him and grilled him trying not to make a scene. "What the fuck are you doing here?" I growled under my breath. "Our business is done. You and my brothers don't even have any more business so why the fuck do you keep showing up?"

"You need to chill before you cause a scene." He warned.

I lowered my voice a little more but my tone was like a growling pit-bull. "You got everything you wanted. Kim is dead and you have your son right? You didn't even know George like that. You just wanna be in my face to be a constant reminder." I frowned.

He shook his head and placed the flowers in my hand. "Don't flatter yourself kidd."

Stepping around me, he made his way to my mama as my eyes followed him. I searched the room for Trey, he was nowhere to be found, which was an indication that he must've been in the back somewhere."

"This is getting so weird." Abbey walked up on the side of me. "Majestic gives me the creeps."

I sucked my teeth and walked away from her not wanting to be bothered all-of-a-sudden. She could entertain Emily and Karter. I just couldn't do it. I needed to get away from here. I found Trey in the back emptying out the cooler. "Wussup ma?" He said putting all the extra sodas in the smaller cooler. "Yo mama workin' a nigga like a runaway slave in this bitch. You okay?"

Trey searched my eyes trying to read me. I tried hard to disguise my attitude.

"I'm ready to go bae. Can we leave?"

Trey stopped what he was doing and walked up on me placing his strong hands on the small of my back pulling me closer to him. "You sure you aiight?" He asked with a seriousness on in his eyes. "We can go if you want, but you sure you ain't got shit to tell me right?" He asked.

"Are you referring to Majestic?" I asked with a raised brow.

"All you gotta do is give me the word."

"It's nothing, I promise." I lied using my right hand to caress his cheek. I then reached up on my toes and kissed him on his full lips. I knew Trey's ass was crazy. He was too calm about wanting to do something to Majestic. "I'm just ready to go." I told him again.

"Come on."

"No." I stopped him. "Let's go through the back. I don't wanna run into nobody. I'm just not in the mood."

Again, he gave me a disapproving look but he respected my wishes. When we got to his truck I slid down into the butter leather seat. "I'm not going to home. You mind if I go with you?" I asked him hoping he wouldn't mind.

He focused on the road and responded. "You aint even gotta ask me no shit like that ma. You already know."

On the way to his house, Abbey was blowing my phone up but I didn't answer. Just like them, I needed time to myself some times as well. When we arrived at Trey's house, I headed straight for his room since it was either there or his one couch. I was so sad I didn't know what to do with myself. I kept stripped down to my panties and bra and got under his covers with tears burning my eyes. Poor Trey didn't know what to do. He tried to cater to my every need but it was killing me. Finally, he laid down with me and spooned me from the back just holding me. I knew that he probably had shit to do since he was always handling business, and I appreciated him changing his plans around for me. Somewhere down the line I dozed off. At this point in time, there was nowhere else in the world I rather had been besides in his arms.

Chapter 12

Kimberly Laws

POW!

The sound of the gunshot that LeLe fired right past my head replayed in my mind over and over as I waited to meet my creator with visions of my son in my mind. I hadn't seen him since the day that Majestic allowed his mama to come and take him away. I saw the clear vision of what was going on. Majestic wanted me out of the picture so him and his mama could raise my baby. He claimed he loved him so much but he hadn't gotten him one time to allow me to see him out of spite. In the matter of weeks, I had been broken down in the worst way. I could still hear LeLe's last words to me. I remember the conversation between her and Majestic and how she convinced Majestic that she would kill me. I really thought she was. When that shot rang off, I knew I was dead. My entire life flashed before my eyes. Everything that I had been through from the time that I was little up until those point had rang out. If I never got to see my son again, I prayed that he would have a happy life, much happier than mine had been.

POW!

The shot replayed in my mind again causing me to jump. I squeezed my eyes shut and said a quick prayer. When I opened my eyes however, I was still on my knees with my back turned, my hands cuffed in front of me and very much alive. I heard the grass crunching under LeLe's shoes as she got closer to me until she was right in front of me staring me in the face with tears in her eyes. "You're not even worth a bullet Kim. You're not worth me losing everything all over again. I'm warning you, go get your son and fucking disappear. Don't ever show your fucking face around here again, or next time, I will surely kill you." She spat looking at me with pity before she jogged off leaving me alone in the dark. I didn't know where Majestic was at this point but I stood up and took off. I ran until I couldn't run anymore. I ran until I saw an busy highway and damn near killed myself trying to run across it and into the lobby of a 'Motel 6'.

I cried the entire way. I cried for my life. I cried for my son. I cried because LeLe had an heart that I can only wish to have one day. I knew Majestic thought that I was dead and I had to keep it this way but I couldn't leave here without my son. I didn't have a phone. I didn't have money. I didn't even have my identification card or my purse for that matter. If they found me dead right now I would be a Jane Doe. If it wasn't for the very helpful hotel manager seeing me in distress, and helping me. I would surely be somewhere dead. She took me to be a victim of domestic violence and offered me a room after I begged her not to call the police. I promised her I needed a few days to get my thoughts together. For the first day, I slept. The second day, I was able to shower and put on a pair of clean jeans and a shirt that 'Maria' the manager had gotten for me. She was also nice enough to get me a pair of knock off sneakers but I didn't give a shit. Since I didn't know anybody's number by heart I couldn't even call. I spent those days strategizing and eating room service although I picked over the majority of the food.

It wasn't until the morning of the third day that I finally left after thanking her for everything. I didn't have anywhere that I could go, but the only person that popped in my mind was Abbey. I needed to get back to Orlando but not without my baby. I was getting him even if I had to steal him back from Ms. Jones. I didn't know how Abbey felt about me since I hadn't seen her since we got back from Orlando together after she beat me up but I was hoping that she had a little love left for me in her heart. I had to hitch hike to North Miami and pray like hell none of the men that gave me rides were rapist. As fucked up as I looked, they probably didn't want to touch me anyway. I walked the few blocks from where I was let out at to Abbey's house making sure that the hoodie I was wearing was tight over my head disguising me since I didn't want to be recognized by anybody. By the time I made it to Abbey's house, I was hot, I was sweating, I was thirsty and I was drained.

Her car wasn't home and that instantly worried me. I knew she had a washroom out back so I walked around to her back porch and let myself in the washroom. There was also a sink in there where I washed my hands and then cupped the palms of my hands under the water and then bringing it to my mouth. Removing the hoodie, I took a deep breath and leaned up against the wall before sliding down onto the floor with my hands on both sides of my face. Every few minutes I would go and check to see if Abbey was home, but she wasn't. The sun was setting and it would be dark soon but I had nowhere to go so I stayed until I fell asleep in her washroom.

A few hours later and well into the night, I woke up and pulled myself off of the floor. I slowly crept to the front to see if Abbey's car was home and it was. Hers along with Trell's. There was a noise coming from the living room. Well actually it sounded like somebody was having some bomb ass sex. From the crack in the blinds, since she didn't have them all the way closed; I could see her on the couch riding Trell's dick like a rodeo star. Her titties bounced up and down while he held her hips. They talking all kinda nasty ass talk to each other that I didn't care to repeat. I pierced my lips together and furrowed my brows. For a brief second, I thought Abbey may have seen me because she looked in my direction causing me to hurry up and duck before making my way back to the washroom. I decided to wait it out. I didn't wanna fuck her little session up and I didn't wanna involved Trell in this. I'd come this far and patience was a virtue.

I thought I was in the clear until I heard the backdoor unlocking. I slid on the side of the washer trying to hide when I saw Trell walk out with his gun in his hand. Abbey clung on to him wearing a robe. "I swear to God I'm not tripping Trell." She whispered. "I saw somebody at the window."

He sucked his teeth after looking around. "Nah ma, you bein' paranoid as fuck. Ain't nobody here. I didn't see shit."

She mushed his head. "That's cause you was busy watching my ass bouncing all over you. I'm telling you, if that bitch Liyah is stalking my house I'mma whoop her ass."

Who the fuck is Liyah? I thought to myself.

"Nah, she know better." He shook his head turning around to go back in. "Come on man. Let me pour you a drink cause you trippin'. Done fucked up my whole vibe."

"Whatever." She mumbled as they both disappeared back inside of the house together.

I sighed a sigh of relief and was glad that I didn't get caught back here. Abbey was the only one I trusted right now. I tried to wait until I heard Trell's car leave but he never did and I was running out of time. In the wee hours of the morning, I realized that he wasn't leaving so I didn't have a choice besides to take a chance. I crept to Abbey's room window. Trell appeared to be in the bed knocked out but no Abbey. I crept to the kitchen because the light was on and figured she may have been in there and sure enough that's where she was. Sipping on a personal bottle of wine. I didn't wanna scare her but I lightly knocked on the window causing her to jump. "What the hell?" She frowned and walked over to the window slightly opening the blinds. When she saw me, her eyes got big as hell. She lift the window up opening it. "Kim?!!!"

"Shhhh." I placed one finger to my mouth looking around.

"Ain't no shush. What are you doing here?" She asked looking over her shoulder. "I thought you were dead. I thought Majestic did something to you." She said with tears in her eyes. "Omg. I can't believe you are here."

She was so busy rambling that I had to wait for her to stop talking. "I need your help Kim." I told her sounding desperate. "Please, but Trell can't know."

She furrowed her brows. "Help for what Kim? What's wrong? I'm so confused right now."

"I can explain. Can you just put something on and come on? Let's take a ride. I'll explain it."

She looked over her shoulder again before looking back at me. "Okay, I'm coming. Meet me at the car."

I did as I was told and just like she promised. Ten minutes later, she came walking out of the house making sure not to make too much noise when she locked the front door. I assumed not wanting to wake Trell up. Gone was her robe and she was wearing a black jogger suit with a pair of black air forces. She hit the unlock button and we got in the car. As soon as she pulled off she started bombarding me with questions. Since I needed her help, I explained everything to her from the beginning up until this point. "Wait, so LeLe was supposed to kill you but she let you go?" She asked for clarification.

"Yes."

"And Majestic thinks you're dead? Like he thinks she did it?"

I nod my head. "Yes."

"He gave your baby to his mama to raise too? After humiliating you the way he did?"

"Yes."

She just stared at me after that. "You look like shit Kim. That's a lot of shit and I don't wish that on my worst enemy." She told me. "What do you want me to help you with?"

"I need you to help me to get my son back without Majestic knowing. I have to get him from Majestic's mama but without her knowing because if I approach her she's going to know I'm alive and she's going to tell him.

Abbey gripped her steering wheel so hard that her knuckles started turning white. She took a long deep breath. "Kim, if I help you with this, you better stay the fuck out of Miami, this is it."

"I'm done with this place. I've been done. I swear." I assured her.

"Where's your car?" She asked.

I shrugged. "I don't know, Majestic probably drove it into the rock pit. I only know it's gone. I just don't know where."

She shook her head. "I can't believe I'm about to do this but every child deserves a mother. Don't ever ask me to do no shit like this again Kim." She warned me.

"I need one more thing." I said to her. "I need a few dollars to catch the mega bus back to Orlando, a shower, and some clean clothes."

I could tell she was thinking about it. "I can help you with that. If you get caught up don't mention my name."

"I would never. Thank you so much." I told her. Abbey knew exactly how to get to Majestic's mama's house. We didn't have a plan, but we were getting the baby.

Chapter 13

Kimberly Laws

"What are you gonna do Kim?" Abbey asked me when we rode by.

We can park on the side of the road. "I'm getting my damn baby." I told her pulling the hoodie back over my head. "I'll be right back. Keep the car running." I told her.

I jogged up to the front door. Since it was still in the early morning hours, it was still dark outside. I walked around the house first to see if I could get a glimpse of them or to see if I heard a noise. Sure enough, my baby boy was up whining and probably wanted a bottle. I felt like I wanted to vomit. I wanted to wrap my arms around him so badly. I wanted to kiss him and hug him never letting go. I can't believe these people were okay with him not being with his own mother. Ms. Jones could say what she wanted. At the end of the day, she was gonna ride with her son no matter what. I was thinking about how I could actually get in the house but as God is my witness, he must've been on my side.

Like magic, the front door opened prompting me to hide behind the bush. Ms. Jones clung on to her robe as she walked out to the garbage with a shitty diaper in her hand getting ready to throw it away. I took that time to dash in the house making sure that my face was covered and my hoodie was far over my head. I had such an adrenaline rush as I scouted the three-bedroom house searching for my baby. There he was in her room in the middle of her bed on his back wrapped up in a blanket. When I saw his face. I forgot about everything that had happened. He was the only thing that mattered as I grabbed him and a few pampers along with the baby bag that sat on her dresser. I rushed out of the room realizing that she was coming back inside of the house. I had to get past her in order to get outside.

In the dark I could imagine I looked like some kind of robber or some kind of kidnapper. Ms. Jones saw me clinging on to the baby and started to scream. "Who are you! Give me my damn grandchild!" She looked scared as shit trying to block the doorway. I made sure my head was low as I shoved my way past her causing her to take a fall on the hard floor. She was yelling to the top of her lungs screaming for help and for someone to call the police. I ran full speed to Abbey's car down the street.

"Get in!" She rushed slapping on the steering wheel. "Let's go! Hurry!" She looked scared as hell and pulled off burning rubber when I made it inside of the car. I was crying and shaking so badly that I couldn't even control it. "I gotta get you out of here Asap Kim. I'm taking you to the mega bus now. We don't have any time to waste!" She warned.

I silently cried and pulled my baby close to me as Abbey sped to the mega bus station. She pulled out her phone when we got there and called Karter. "Karter!" She yelled her name in the phone breathing all hard and shit like she had just run a marathon. "I found Kim okay? And she's coming home! I don't have time to explain but I'm putting her and the baby on the bus now. She'll be there in three hours so make sure she has a ride when she gets there." She told her as I listened.

When she hung up, she pulled out her wallet and gave me a hundred dollar bill. "This all I got on me right now but that should be all that you need okay?"

I grabbed the money and stuffed it down in my pocket. "Thank you so much." I told Abbey and grabbed the baby bag with my heart racing. She hopped out so she could use her debit card to go and purchase my ticket and she made me wait until she got back. When she did, we got out before hugging. Abbey watched me and the baby until we were loaded on the bus and pulling off. From the window, I look at her again and saw all the worry on her face. Again, I thanked her with my eyes until she was no longer in my eyesight. I stared down at my baby's face and sighed. It was at this moment that I realized there was nothing that I wouldn't do for him. I was truly sorry for Ms. Jones and Majestic's loss when it came to Malik, but Junior was too perfect for them. He was just an innocent baby that shouldn't be used for a pawn. Majestic didn't even have time for him self. I knew he wouldn't be able to put in the time to raise a little baby.

At this point, I had paid for my sins. I didn't realize until now how strong I really was. I would lose my life for my child. I had been humiliated in the worst way and I was still standing. I didn't need a drug to help me cope. That's when I knew a little faith could take you a long way. I closed my eyes and took the three-hour ride until I was back in my safe haven. I truly hoped everything would be fine. Ms. Jones didn't see my face, she didn't know who could've took the baby and because they technically stole him from me, they couldn't even call the police. Fuck them all. When we arrived in Orlando, Emily and Karter was waiting on us along with baby Barbie as well. One look at me and they knew something wasn't right. I knew I looked rough and one could tell I had been through some shit. They had so many questions for me that I simply didn't wanna answer. I finally just broke down and let it all out allowing the tears to fall as I balled my eyes out in both of there arms. They had been here for me in more ways than imaginable.

When they finally took me home, the place was spotless and it was like I never left. Warm and welcoming. After I showered and gave the baby a bath. I sipped a cup of hot tea and then told them the story. I told them everything but I made sure to leave LeLe's name out of it. She had been through enough. I didn't wanna tarnish her name or drag her. I had taken life away from her and in return, she allowed me to live. I wouldn't be breathing right now if it wasn't for LeLe. Me mentioning her was simply off of limits.

Chapter 14

Leandra 'LeLe' Wells

I had been at Trey's house for a few days ignoring the outside world and trying to get my mind together. You never know how differently shit affects people. The only person I had spoken with was my mama. I hadn't even spoken to my brothers or Abbey and she had been calling me like crazy. I rolled over and got out of the bed. My body had been so sore as well from Trey fucking me in every position that my body would allow. I could truly get used to this. I made my way to the bathroom and brushed my teeth with the toothbrush he had brought here for me. I had a few clothes as well that we had stepped out together to get a few days ago. "Bae!" I yelled from the bathroom. He didn't answer so I rinsed my mouth out and the walked out of the room to find him as my feet glided over his cold tile floors. I found him in the kitchen fully dressed in a Balenciaga fit from head to toe wondering where he was going.

Trey looked the fuck good. The man woke up looking good. Went to sleep looking good. Some times I felt as if he was just simply too good to be true. Everybody who may have thought he was faking by being so low key, I could honestly say he was like this in real life. He didn't fuck with other people outside of his family. Those are the only people I ever heard him talking to outside of business. Especially his cousin Gu, that was his real right hand man. It was never Cass like we all initially thought. "What up sleepin' beauty." He signaled for me to come to him.

I made my way over to him and stood in between his legs since he was sitting at the barstool. I looked around. I loved being at his house but it was so damn bland.

He really needed a woman's touch in here. "Good morning." I kissed him on the lips. He smelled so good.

"Morning." He replied. He was reading a book called 'the secret' but he closed it to give me his undivided attention. "I got you something." He pulled a box from his pocket and gave it to me.

"What's this?" I asked with a huge smile on my face. "You know you don't have to get me things right? I'm not materialistic like that Trey."

"And that's why I don't mind doin' shit for you. I don't splurge ma, but if I ever give you something it's gone always have a meaning behind it." He schooled me chuckling.

"What?" I asked checking my breath hoping it wasn't foul. I had washed it pretty good.

"You women are a trip. You gone take the gift anyway cause ya'll like that kind of shit. Ion know what woman doesn't."

"Whatever." I said pulling the chain from the box. It was a small white diamond necklace. The round pendant that hung from it had a picture of George. The same picture that we used in his obituary. "Awww." My eyes watered up. "I love this. This is so beautiful. So he can always be close to my heart. Aww Trey I love it!" I wrapped my arms around him giving him a hug. "You're so good to me."

He grabbed the chain to put it around my neck. "As long as you don't switch up on me. I wont ever switch up on you shorty." He told me. "Come here." When I turned around he kissed me softly on the lips.

"I love you!" I blurted damn near scaring myself. I didn't mean to say it. It was like my tongue had a mind of it's own the way it just so comfortably rolled off. I was so scared. I dropped my eyes. "I um… I'm sorry." I apologized.

Trey grabbed me by my waist forcing me to look in his eyes. "You ain't gotta apologize ma. Stop apologizing for how you feel. That's like apologizing for being real." He then looked at me side ways. "So what it's gone be? You love me, or you don't? She loves me, or she loves me not." He gave me that sexy smirk.

I had to take a second to evaluate my own feelings. Did I love Trey? I had to because why did I just so easily say that. I guess it did love him. What terrified me was loving after the pain. I realized I had to let go of all of that and it was time. I nod my head staring into his eyes. "Yes baby, I love you." I told him.

"Good, cause I love you too shorty." He told me making sure he looked into my eyes when he told me that. "I loved you since the day I laid eyes on you in Jazzy's when you first got out of prison and that shit wouldn't ever go nowhere ma. This where we at now and it's only up from here."

Trey made me fall in love with him every second on the second. "That's good to know. You make me so happy."

"Same here." He let me know.

"What you doing today?" I asked.

"Check on my properties. The usual. "What you got going on?" He asked.

"Well first I'mma go get some damn groceries to put in this damn house and then I'mma go to the restaurant and cook you a good ass meal. Meet me there tonight."

"I can do that. Nigga want some steak, garlic shrimp, garlic butter potatoes, some asparagus and some sweet cornbread. "I'm a country nigga baby. Can you handle that?" He placed his hand on his stomach.

"Damnnn all of that?" I joked.

He nod his head. "Yep, allat. Can you handle it?"

"Now you know I can handle it." I told him before walking away to go get myself together. "I need you to take me to my car!" I yelled over my shoulder.

"I got you." His deep voice boomed through the walls.

I kissed Trey one more time before he let me out at my house before pulling off. When I walked inside of the house. I was alone, nobody was here and it felt weird as fuck being in this house knowing that George was never gonna walk through these doors ever again. I felt like I was about to have an anxiety attack. I rushed to gather my things and ran out of the house after locking up. When I pulled off I went to the grocery store and racked up on some groceries to put in Trey's house. I would have to just store his bags in the fridge at the restaurant until I was able to get them to his house. I loved being in my place of business and my grand opening was a week away. I was too excited and had a lot of special recipes and meals that I wanted everyone to get a taste of. I had a new mac and cheese recipe that would make a nigga wanna slap his mama.

As soon as I started prepping the food for Trey, Abbey called me once again. "Bitch! Where the fuck have you been LeLe? You just drop off the face of the fucking earth and don't call nobody when I'm in the middle of a fucking crisis!"

"What crisis?" I asked. "Cause if it's got shit to do with Trell I don't wanna hear it."

"Trell and me are beyond good. Our thing is our thing. Now where the fuck are you? We need to talk asap!"

"I'm at LeLe's." I told her wondering what could be so important. "If you wanna talk then hurry up cause I have a date." I didn't want her to be here when Trey arrived. I wanted her to be long gone.

Within a few minutes, Abbey was knocking on the door and I had to unlock it to let her in. She followed me back to the kitchen where I continued working. "So what's up?" I asked.

She tapped her freshly manicured nails on the counter in front of me. "So you were supposed to kill Kim and you didn't?"

"Okay, and how do you know that?" I stopped chopping the onions waiting for an answer. Nobody was supposed to know that. Well, at least not Majestic.

"Because she came to me for help LeLe. I helped her kidnap her baby back and now she's gone back to Orlando."

I didn't know where this was going. "Okay so what's the problem?" I asked.

She sighed. "The problem is, you should've at least kept me in the loop on what was going on with her. She's still my fucking friend!"

"And so am I!" I reminded her. "Whose side are you on anyway? I didn't tell you to keep you out of that shit! That's why you didn't know. I didn't ask you to go and make yourself a fucking accomplice." I frowned and started back cutting the onions. "She's a fucked up person, but she didn't deserve to die. Majestic is just a sick son of a bitch."

Abbey turned around looking over her shoulder. "Did you hear something?" She asked.

"No." I replied. "Did you lock the door back?"

She sucked her teeth. "Damn, ion think so. Let me go see."

When Abbey walked away. I grabbed the green onions to start chopping those as well. "Nope! I don't see anybody! Guess I just was hearing shit!" She yelled from the front.

I thought I was tripping when I felt somebody staring at me but when I turned around I didn't see anybody. I shrugged just as Abbey came walking back in the kitchen. "So are you mad?" I asked. "Is that what all this is about?"

She grabbed her keys and her purse. "No that's not what I'm saying LeLe." She rolled her eyes. "You just need to work on your communication skills that's all. This shit was deeper than rap and you didn't even put me on. You knew I was worried about Kim. You could've at least told me that she was still alive and okay."

I didn't wanna keep having this discussion with Abbey. I had done my good deed by letting her live. I was ready for all this shit to be over now. If it was anything I had learned it was the fact that life was way too short. I followed Abbey to the front door and let her out. I didn't bother to lock it back because I knew that Trey was coming soon. It didn't take me any time to finish cooking and the place was lit up. It smelled so good. I walked over to the tables and lit some candles and then played a slow jam from the jukebox. When I walked back to the back to place the food on plates, I nearly shitted on myself when I felt the cold steel on the bag of my head. My hands flew up in the air and my heart dropped. "I don't keep no money here." I said with quivering lips thinking I was being robbed.

He chuckled. "Bitch I don't need yo fucking money."

I knew that damn voice, it was Majestic. I knew I was in trouble and if he was coming after me, it was for one thing.

"Majestic...I..." I couldn't even get the words out.

"Shut the fuck up bitch. I always knew you was a fuckin' snake just like I called it. I couldn't figure out for the life of me who the fuck would wanna steal my baby. All the babies in the world and a muhfucka just wanted to take mine huh? So then I got to thinking and shit. It was only one person who wanted that baby more than anything else. My mind didn't want me to believe it, but I had to check anyway so I drove back to the spot I had reserved for Kim's sour ass body and to my surprise; the hole I buried was empty. Just as empty as when I dug it out."

"I'm not a fucking killer Majestic. That girl did some shit but she didn't deserve to die."

"I should've killed you when I had the fuckin' chance." He growled cocking the gun.

I closed my eyes and took a deep breathe imagining that this is what Kim felt like when she thought I was gonna shoot her. I couldn't do shit besides pray. If he was gonna take my life, at least I had managed to accomplish something and leave something with my name on it behind me. Just when I thought I was getting my life back, here he was wanting to take it. I was just too tired. If God loved me so much, he wouldn't keep pulling me back down. I took a deep breathe. "If you gonna kill me, then just kill me." I told him.

Within the blink of an eye, everything happened so fast. I remember Trey appearing in the doorway with his gun already out. I remembered Majestic grabbing me from behind while aiming his own gun at Trey. I remember me ducking right before the bullet rang out. I was under the counter screaming as Trey and Majestic had a full shoot out in my kitchen. I tried to run to get closer to Trey. Big Mistake. The burning sensation I felt in my shoulder was undeniable. "Get down LeLe!" Trey growled. At the same time Majestic's body fell next to me on the floor with a bullet pierced through his forehead. The way his lifeless eyes stared back at me caused me to faint. Between that and all the blood pouring from my shoulder, I was positive that I was gonna day. Trey ran over to me right before everything went black.

I truly couldn't take anymore. When I came to again, I was in the hospital with everyone surrounding me. Trey was right next to me. "Am I dead?" I asked in excruciating pain.

"You ain't dead baby girl." Trey told me looking worried. "You took a hit to the shoulder but they gone watch you over night. you gone be aiight." He told me.

My mama was on the side of me stroking my hair and Abbey, Trell, and Leon along with Kevin were standing around the bed as well. My brothers looked hurt. They looked pissed as well. "Thank you for watchin' out for my sister man." Trell told Trey. "A nigga forever in depth to you for that shit. If I could bring that nigga back and kill him again I would."

"Don't talk like that." My mama scolded him. Abbey and me just locked eyes and I knew she was glad that I was okay. I closed my eyes and tried to doze back off. I quickly opened my eyes back.

"What about my restaurant?" I cried. "I know it's ruined."

"Don't worry about that. Just get better, we got it covered." Trey told me.

"Are you gonna go to jail Trey? You killed that man! He's dead."

"Not for self defense I'm not. I would've been locked up by now ma. Just rest." He told me again. I decided to close my eyes and do just that. Whatever was gonna happen, I had to let run it's course.

Chapter 15

Abbey Daniels

For the past few weeks we had all come together working diligently around the clock to get LeLe's restaurant back in order but we did it. We all came together to make sure her opening night was everything and more. Trell and me were at my house getting dressed one minute and the next, I was sitting on the toilet reading a positive pregnancy test. I couldn't believe it. Never in a million years could I say I was truly prepared for this. Trell had just gotten a job at UM and he finally got that coaching job as well. Everything was going up from here but now here I was with another problem and we didn't need a baby. At the same time, I didn't wanna abort either.

"Abbey!" He knock on the bathroom door. "We gone be late bae come on!"

"I can't!" I yelled back.

"You can't what?"

"I can't come out Trell!" I sighed.

"The fuck does that mean?!" He asked sounding confused.

I literally felt like I was stuck to the toilet but I said fuck it and marched to the door swinging it open with worried tears in my eyes. I just knew my face was flushed. I just blurted it out. "You're gonna be a daddy Trell." I held the test up to his face dangling it.

He snatched it from me and stared at it with a huge smile on his face. "You foreal? Don't be fucking with me Abbey. Is this real?" He asked still smiling.

"Yes Trell."

"Well why you crying then? Are you happy? I'm happy ma."

"I'm happy and scared at the same time." I told him.

"Well if you scared you don't gotta be. I'mma be here wit'chu and I'm not goin' nowhere. That's a promise, It's up from here. We got this." He kissed me with a big hug making me feel so much better.

"Thank you Trell. That mean so much to me. We came a long ass way."

"We did ma. Let's roll so we can celebrate."

Trell and me walked out dressed in 'LeLe's Place' shirts so we could help out when we got there. We all had a job tonight. When we arrived the place was packed waiting for the ribbon cutting. LeLe's arm was still in a sling but she looked beautiful and happy wearing a glow. A glow that I hadn't seen since she was with Malik. I stood next to Trey after greeting everybody and gave him a hug. "Thank you so much for making my friend happy bringing life back into her." I smiled.

"I wouldn't have it no other way." He hugged me back.

When it was time for the ribbon cutting we all celebrated. There were photographers, there was a DJ, the local radio station and all kinds of people from near and far. I knew LeLe was gonna be busy but when I found her with a little bit of down time. I told her how proud of her I was. "I'm so happy for you friend." I hugged her. "You did the damn thing. This is everything." I beamed.

"Thank you so much best friend. It's been along time coming and I can say I'm genuinely happy. This is the happiest I've been in a long ass time. Everything that I dreamed of is coming true." She beamed.

"Yep, and you're glowing too bitch. That's that happy glow."

"You're glowing yourself." She told me looking me up and down. "I'm glad that Trell is sticking to his word and making you happy. I'm glad you two love each other. It's a beautiful thing."

A huge smile spread across me face. "So we finally have your blessing?"

She nod her head. "Yeah, ya'll got my blessing."

I decided to tell her my news. "Good, because you're going to be an aunt." I touched my stomach. "Shhh I don't want anybody else to know right now."

LeLe's eyes lit up. "Whattt? Omg are you foreal? Ya'll having a baby?" She cried. "Wowwww. Congrats." She hugged me again just as Trell and the rest of the crew walked over.

"What ya'll over here gossiping about?" Kevin asked.

"Nothing but good vibes only." I beamed. "In due time, you all will know." I winked my eye at Trell as he wrapped his arms around me.

LeLe grabbed Trey by the hand and looked him in the eyes. "I just want to say thank you again. In case I don't thank you enough baby."

"I'm doin' my job ma. Nigga love you. I'm proud of you." He kissed my lips.

"Get a fuckin' room." Leon joked.

Kevin playfully slapped his arm. "Leave them alone bae. They are so cute." He smiled.

We all took a moment to reflect on how life was at this moment. Everything we went through was supposed to happen this way. Our stories were already written. It took for things to happen to get to this point. When Mrs. Wells walked over to us she had more joy on her face than I'd seen in weeks. "What all my children over here talking about? Ya'll sho keep me going."

"We got you forever ma." Trell told her.

We all agreed knowing that George was smiling down on us. I watched LeLe hold the picture of George that was on her necklace around her neck and rub her finger across it. "Ya'll hold hands real quick. Let's pray." Mrs. Wells said.

We didn't oblige, we all came together and did as we were told. She started. *"Help family members to be at peace with one another. Manifest your divine love within' their hearts and let your tranquility be bestowed in their lives. In Jesus' name, I rebuke every thought of hatred, malice and pride towards one another and every dispute and argument in our homes, Lord. Thank you for your strength, your peace, and your lead. Amen."*

"Amen." We all said in unison.

I was so glad everything was for once on one accord but there was still something I needed to do. I snuck away and called Kim. "Hey Kim. How are you and the baby? I just wanted to check on ya'll."

"Hey Abbey." She spoke sounding in much better spirits. "How are you? I was just heading to bible study with the baby."

"I know he's getting big huh?" I smiled.

"Yes." She cooed. "I love him so much."

"Well I'm glad you're doing better. I just wanted to check on you. The New Year is approaching so just in case I don't get to speak with you I want to wish you a happy new year."

"Same to you babes. Same to you. It's been so hard." She said as her voice started cracking. "Lord knows but if there's a will there's a way. I'm just happy and thank God for change. If they ever said a person couldn't change. I'm a living testimony to that."

"Yeah…" I stared off. "I guess you are. I love you girl."

"I love you too." She told me. "Abbey can you do me a favor?" She asked.

"Sure." I replied. "What's up."

"When you get a chance, tell LeLe that I said thank you. I could only wish to be half of the woman that she has become. She is truly one of a kind. I know I'll never be accepted again but the love will never change. Please take care of each other." She told me.

I had to get off the phone before Kim had me crying and shit. "Will do baby girl. Will do. Until next time Kim. You take care of you and that beautiful baby."

"I sure will." She told me before hanging up.

I turned around and wiped my eyes before heading back inside. This was a new beginning for us all. No pain, no gain. What didn't kill us only made us stronger and a family in union was better than an family divided. I wished for only peace and blessings. It was only up from here. I said a silent prayer to myself for the Lord to continue to wrap his arms around us. I knew moving forward, we had this. New babies and new money from here on out and nothing could stop us. I said it so many times already. We were all the way up!

The End.

CPSIA information can be obtained
at www.ICGtesting.com
Printed in the USA
LVHW081744280220
648532LV00010B/698